SECRETS MADE
IN PARADISE

SECRETS MADE IN PARADISE

NATALIE ANDERSON

MILLS & BOON

First published in Great Britain 2020
by Mills & Boon, an imprint of HarperCollins*Publishers*
1 London Bridge Street, London, SE1 9GF

Large Print edition 2021

© 2020 Natalie Anderson

ISBN: 978-0-263-08985-1

MIX
Paper from
responsible sources
FSC
www.fsc.org
FSC C007454

This book is produced from independently certified FSC™ paper to ensure responsible forest management. For more information visit www.harpercollins.co.uk/green.

Printed and bound in Great Britain
by CPI Group (UK) Ltd, Croydon, CR0 4YY

For my Friday Coffee Crew—
love you guys :)

CHAPTER ONE

JAVIER TORRES IGNORED the paperwork strewn across his lap and gazed out of the tinted window of the SUV, absently watching his driver walk into the small store to stock up on refreshments. It was late afternoon, the weather was glorious, and he ought to feel like a king. He was back on the threshold of paradise— Santa Cruz, the most populated of the Galapagos islands and arguably one of the planet's most isolated and fascinating places. He was here to oversee the start of the hotel rebuild he'd recently invested in. Yet instead of feeling satisfied, he was distracted by an uneasy, prickling sensation. No matter how hard he tried, he couldn't shake the recollection of the last time he'd been here. More precisely, the redhead he'd ravished. There really wasn't any other word for what had transpired between them. But she'd ravished him right back— with such rare intensity that she'd haunted his dreams every night of the eighteen months since.

It wasn't as if he'd never had a one-night stand before. It was pretty much all he had. *She* hadn't though. A wisp of wicked amusement flickered through him as he remembered there'd been a number of firsts for her that night. She'd been travelling, all the way from Australia, and who knew where in the world she was now? Certainly not Javier. She'd not been there when he'd woken the next morning and he'd had to return to mainland Ecuador that evening in time to catch his flight home to New York.

It wasn't supposed to matter. He'd not meant to care. Only he'd been unable to forget. Searing memories tormented his nights and teased in unwanted, unsummoned daydreams. Javier had rarely daydreamed before meeting her. And the impact she'd had on his sex life was frankly appalling. He was stuck in the longest ever stretch of abstinence. He told himself it was because he was busy with work projects and plans. In reality no woman he'd met since had aroused him. It was infuriating. He could do with a fantastic, physical night of unfettered pleasure; the stress release would be good and being back on this island only brought those memories to the fore even more.

And just like that she appeared—walking out of the shop—an erotic vision with her stunning solar-flare-red hair and fantastically generous curves. Javier groaned. Of course his tormented mind would conjure her here. It was the ultimate in wishful thinking and the craving was so strong he simply sank back into the seat, helpless to do anything other than enjoy the mirage. His skin tightened as his muscles surged at the sight of her lush body. That first night he'd seen her before she'd seen him and the artless confidence with which she'd walked from the water, bold in her bright green bikini and owning her space, had made her the sexiest thing he'd ever seen. Now she turned as a young couple followed her out of the store. She pointed something out down the road and the other woman handed her a phone. The couple posed beside the store sign while the redhead took their picture. Then the redhead turned as Javier's driver emerged from the shop. He sent her a massive smile. Of course he did, who wouldn't when passing a woman that stunning? But all this interaction meant she wasn't a hallucination.

The universe went mute. Javier didn't blink or breathe. His heart didn't beat. He stared intently, watching her walk in those slightly too snug jeans that strained to contain her gorgeously shapely hips and thighs. His mouth dried. Her loose khaki linen shirt was unbuttoned, revealing a white tank top beneath, giving the merest, most tantalising glimpse of her other blessedly bountiful curves. And that glorious riot of red was barely holding up in a half-tumbling topknot, revealing her high cheekbones and freckled skin. Every muscle clenched at the sight of her intensely feminine frame while the memory of her soft, silken heat consumed him.

His driver opened the door.

'Wait a moment, please,' Javier instructed hoarsely.

The redhead's smile had just gone nuclear. Javier's tension sky-rocketed and he turned to see who warranted such a warm welcome. His burst of strain was soothed as he saw an elderly woman slowly walking along the path. She was carrying a baby—a dark-haired, smiling bundle who stretched his tiny arms out and wriggled impatiently as he saw the redhead run towards them.

Noise returned in a jangling cacophony, pummelling Javier as he watched the reunion. He drew a sharp breath while his brain whirred—registering that relationship, calculating the passage of time with precision, computing the shocking combination of facts in a nanosecond and coming up with a conclusion that was utterly appalling.

Cold panic clashed with wild horror. Because he knew with absolute certainty that the redhead *was* the woman he'd seduced all those months ago—Emerald, the sweet siren from that beautiful beach. And that baby was definitely her child. And with equal unequivocal, icy conviction, he knew her child was also *his*.

An awful crevasse opened within, rapidly filling with a hot lava of guilt. She'd had his baby and he'd not known. Because she'd not been able to contact him. Because that night he'd been careless and he'd not told her his true name.

Now he studied her again—not seeing the sexy curves of her body and the striking colour of her hair this time, but the frayed, faded edges of her shirt, the worn patches of her jeans, the strain around her eyes. At the signs of her struggle, that guilt within him grew, as did utter regret for her and for her child.

Children had never been on Javier's *to do* list and, frankly, would never be. As for marriage? Well hell, no. He'd not just witnessed the worst of those intimate wars, he'd been collateral damage. So no, his life was rich enough with work, any instinctive need to leave a mark sated by the creation of his own little business empire, any inner restlessness soothed by travel. He had no need and no desire for deep relationships or emotional responsibilities. The concept of fatherhood was so far from his realm of knowledge it was like a bad joke—how could he possibly do a decent job of parenting when he'd had such a rubbish example in his own life? Well, not a rubbish example, more like *no* example at all.

He'd never wanted some other poor kid to be rejected and neglected the way he had. Yet— albeit inadvertently—he'd done exactly that to his own for months. Anger surged at his incompetence, but so did something primal. The need to protect. And the need to make things right. But that sense of duty wasn't backed up by paternal knowledge or skill. He clenched his jaw, biting back his disappointment in his own failings. He was no hero, but he'd provide what he could, as soon as he could. He just had to figure out the best way how.

Emerald Jones glanced at her watch. Less than twenty minutes and she'd have Luke back. It had only been an hour but she missed him already. Such long shifts at the small store were hard, but she was incredibly grateful for the chance to keep her dignity and her boss, Connie, adored spending some time with Luke in the afternoons. The rest of the time Emmy was able to keep him occupied in a little playpen behind the counter, though she worried she wouldn't be able to for much longer given how adventurous and alarmingly mobile her curious little boy was becoming. That was a problem she was too tired to think of a solution to yet. Honestly? She was surviving one day to the next.

She glanced up as a tall figure stepped through

the shadowed doorway. As he moved into the light a hit of pure exhilaration soared, a leap of joy so powerful she almost cried out with delight. Instead she froze—that sound trapped in her throat.

Eighteen months ago the world had tilted, never returning to rights. Now it tilted again, taking another rotation and rendering everything upside down.

'Ramon?' she breathed.

Dark brown eyes—a decadent mix of cocoa and coffee—stared into her soul. Vaguely she absorbed details—the charcoal linen trousers, the white shirt, the sleeves rolled to three-quarters, revealing tanned, strong forearms—but it was those eyes that stunned her. She trembled from tip to toe with a powerful whole-body reaction. She'd suffered this shudder of raw recognition that first night too. He'd captured every iota of her attention in a way no other person ever had. And look what had happened.

Hormones. Her own chemistry had failed her. Because with another micro blink of time she'd remembered. He wasn't 'Ramon'. He'd deceived her, he'd lied about his identity and his reason for being on the island. *Nothing* had been real. He'd used her so completely. She'd shown him the most perfect place and then he'd stolen it. She hated him for that.

But at the same time, more memories stirred—those secret ones she'd tried to bury. Because while he'd taken the place she loved, she had to admit he hadn't *stolen* that other deeply personal thing from her. She'd given him her body, her virginity, more than freely. In that moment she'd been so willing, and it had been so magical she could never brand it a mistake, despite discovering his dishonesty since. And most importantly, he'd given her something beyond priceless.

Luke.

Her small son. *His* son. The one he knew *nothing* about.

Icy terror destroyed her equilibrium as she realised this man could take *everything*—as quickly and easily as he'd taken her innocence that night. Her heart pounded as the remnants of elation from that unthinking rush of recognition were sucked away by fear and the worst, worst guilt. She should have told him, she *had* to tell him. But not here, not now, not when Luke was due back with Connie at any moment. She needed to get 'Ramon' to leave and she'd tell him later when she'd figured out how...

She should have figured out how already.

'Emmy.' His smile was tight, but still devastating.

She blinked. She didn't want to respond to his looks and charm. Not knowing the truth. Because she'd learned 'Ramon'—her carefree surfer-dude tourist—was really Javier Torres. Billionaire investor. Billionaire playboy. Billionaire *jerk*.

When she'd learned his true identity—a few months after Luke's birth—she'd never wanted to see him again. Her already bruised heart had broken on finding out he was so lacking in integrity. And not only was Javier Torres a man who lied easily, he was terrifyingly powerful. Initially she'd been too angry to contact him, then she'd grown too scared as she'd realised the implications of his assets and while she knew it was wrong, she'd had no choice. Her childhood had been marred by lie after lie. She'd been deceived before, but, worse, *she'd* also been the liar. And when Javier discovered that last? He'd be furious. She knew well that angry people lashed out in a variety of ways. None of them good. Integrity was everything and trust, once lost, wasn't regained. But she couldn't have another dishonest person wreck her life, even if she had to be dishonest herself to keep him out. Because she wasn't having what had happened to her happen to her son.

Yet even as she mentally rejected Javier, she was hit again by that terrible chemistry. That hidden, secret part of her weakened with want. She'd ached for him for months. He'd starred in her dreams night after night after night— indeed *every* night since then.

Feeling sick with guilt, she was conscious of the empty playpen behind her and the ticking clock on the wall. Protecting her son's future—and her own part in it—was paramount.

'It's been a while...' She forced her parched lips into a smile so he wouldn't suspect anything. As far as he knew, she still thought he was 'Ramon'. 'How may I help? Did you want to buy something?'

He didn't take his intense gaze off her. 'No.'

To her horror he was more stunning than she

remembered, with the sort of superhuman good looks that everyone normal couldn't help but stare at. But as she watched him move closer, she realised he'd become sharper. There was a slight shadow beneath his eyes and stubble on his jaw and an edginess about him that was new. Perhaps it was the stress of his business? Were all those wolfish property takeovers designed to amass his personal fortune wearing him out?

The intensity of his gaze strengthened. He'd looked at her this way when he'd seduced her that night—powerfully mesmerising. Yes, there was still that tiny part positively revelling in being in his presence again. Desperately she dragged that wild piece within her back beneath her control. She couldn't let him seduce her again. She couldn't let herself *or* Luke down like that.

'It's been far too long, Emerald,' he said softly. 'Why don't you shut up the shop early?' But his tempting smile didn't quite meet his too attentive eyes. 'Come for a drive with me so we can catch up properly.'

'What?' She froze, shocked by the invitation. Panic tightened her throat. 'I—I can't leave.'

'No? I thought you were a woman of freedom and spontaneity.'

Cold sweat slicked her skin. 'I have work.' And she had Luke. The baby she'd not told him about.

Bile burned the back of her throat, because she was going to have to tell him and she should have already. As soon as she'd discovered his actual identity she should have reached out— there'd been no barrier to finding him *then*. She was, after all, the one determined to live a life of integrity and not follow the path of lies and deceit of her own family. But she'd been too scared of his reaction. Not just to the news he'd had a son, but how he'd react to *her*. She'd been burned before, when people had learned the truth about her background, and she'd been too hurt by his *needless* lie. Why had he needed to fake who he was?

'I never expected to see you here,' he muttered watchfully. 'I imagined you travelling around the world ticking off that bucket list, but have you been in the Galapagos all this time?'

Nervously she swallowed. 'Yes.'

'I didn't realise you worked on the island.'

'It didn't come up in our conversation.' She looked anxiously to the door. Any minute now Connie would arrive with little Luke. 'And I really need to get back to it...'

His smile faded as his whole expression tightened. 'What's the real reason you won't come with me now, Emerald?' he asked quietly.

'What do you mean?' Trepidation slithered over her skin. 'I have work. I'm the only one here, as you can see.'

She felt physically ill at telling half-truths—but what he could do, what he could take...

And then she heard the gurgling chuckle of her beloved little boy. At the next strike of her next hammering heartbeat, Connie appeared in the doorway with Luke in her arms. Emerald's world teetered, about to smash to smithereens and it was entirely her own fault. There was no way to get Connie to turn around, to run and hide Luke. Her only option was to try to fake it through the next few minutes and tell Javier the truth, alone, later, once she'd had a chance to draw breath. She should have come up with a plan months ago. But she'd been too busy caring for Luke. Too busy surviving.

Swallowing the nausea with a fake smile, she tried to act as if nothing horrific was currently happening. 'Thanks, Connie,' she whispered. 'Can you just go upstairs for a moment? I'll be there as soon as I can.'

Connie had stilled. Luke too was abnormally quiet, as if he'd sensed something strange in the atmosphere. The elderly woman glanced curiously at Javier. It was obvious her brain was doing the maths and in this case getting it right. But fortunately she said nothing as she walked past the counter, taking Luke with her.

'Who was that?' Javier asked, the second the elderly woman disappeared up the stairs.

'My boss, Connie.' Emmy could hardly bear to face him, but she forced herself to meet his gaze and her breathing stalled.

Javier was still scrutinising her, his expression sombre. 'I meant the baby,' he explained softly.

Emmy's mind blanked and she stared at him.

'What's his name?' His question was too quiet.

She couldn't think what to answer.

'What is his name, Emmy?' The edge in that repeated question sliced through to her bones.

She gazed up into those achingly familiar brown eyes. She absolutely adored the owner of the smaller set, but these ones held a glint that she couldn't define. A premonition shook her resolve. He'd be steely and unforgiving, but she couldn't lie now. Not to his face. Not the way he had to her.

'His name is Luke.'

'What's his full name?' Javier pressed with unerring precision.

Sweat slicked her skin.

'Didn't you give him a middle name?'

That was when she realised Javier already knew. He *already knew* Luke was his. Terror transfixed her. How long had he known and what had he planned? Because he clearly had something in mind. Him walking into her shop was no moment of chance. She had no idea what to do or say in response—all she knew was that she couldn't trust his handsome visage.

'Lucero Ramon Jones. Isn't that right?' Javier confirmed her fears with dangerously gentle accuracy.

'You've seen his birth certificate?' Her voice barely sounded.

'You left the father's name blank.'

How had he seen that certificate? How long had he been here?

'Emerald?' he prompted.

'For good reason,' she tossed back on a rush of adrenalin and anger. 'I'm not sure who the father is.'

'Are you not?' He cocked his head. 'Emmy, we both know the dates fit. I was your first lover and you've even named him after me.'

Heat surged. 'I named him after the man who *lied* to me. Who didn't even tell me his real name. "Ramon" was nothing but a lie—a fake persona from some entitled sociopath. You're not him.'

He was nothing like the man he'd passed himself off as—funny and charming, carefree yet caring. Javier Torres was none of those things.

For a long moment he was utterly silent, but emotion enlarged his pupils so much that the black-coffee core almost obliterated the cocoa-coloured iris completely.

'What's *my* name, Emmy?' he finally asked in a bloodless, shocked-sounding whisper.

Too late she realised she'd given herself

away. Now he knew that *she* knew he'd lied to her. She straightened, determined to hide her fear because surely, in the shades of grey in this mess, *he* was the worst liar between them? And even if he wasn't, she had to be completely honest now. 'Javier Torres.'

He nodded slowly. 'Javier *Ramon* Torres.'

She closed her eyes. That name had been the only tribute she'd been able to offer her son at the time of his birth. She'd felt so betrayed when she'd learned 'Ramon' was really Javier and humiliated that she'd given it to Luke. But now it was relevant again? It was their common middle name and, while that should be a soothing symmetry, stupidly it hurt her more.

'How long have you known?' His question now had an edge and she couldn't blame him.

'Not long.' She lifted her chin bravely. 'Since the media release about the Flores property.'

The property *she'd* shown him—her most favourite place in the world. Her sanctuary. She'd been naive to share something so special with a stranger. Those moments of lust and excitement had made her brainless. Because he'd bought it and was now transforming it from budget retreat to swanky hotel. He was a brutal, ruthlessly acquisitive business-man. Nothing like the carefree sea god who'd held her spellbound that evening on her precious beach.

'That was months ago.' His mouth compressed. 'Yet you've not got in touch since.'

'You lied to me,' she muttered.

'It seems we're both liars.'

She pushed down her rising panic.

'How could you just try to tell me you didn't know who his father is?' he asked.

'I didn't—not for months anyway and even then I found out little more than your real name.'

'You should have contacted me the second you found that out.'

He was right and yet wrong, because she'd learned more than his real name, she'd discovered his lack of integrity too.

'I don't know *you* at all, nothing other than that you lied to me that night,' she defended herself desperately. 'I couldn't even be completely sure that the jerk written about in the paper was actually the guy from that night.'

Except that was weak of her. She'd glanced at that picture in the paper and known instantly.

'The second I walked in the door just now, you were sure,' he said. 'But you hustled that child upstairs.'

'Maybe that's because I'm *terrified*.' She glared at him, taking a step to widen her stance, wishing she could make a better barrier between him and that stairway.

'Because I present danger to you? To him?' He recoiled. 'Based on what evidence? Was I violent?'

Her throat tightened but she forced the truth to whisper out. 'No.'

'Then what have I done to hurt you? If I remember correctly, *you* were the one who walked out without so much as a goodbye.'

The flash of reproach in his eyes deepened her guilt.

'Why did you leave so early?' he added. 'Why not wake me to say goodbye? Were you *that* full of regret?'

'No,' she muttered, hoarse with burning embarrassment.

'You could have left a note.'

'What was the point? I thought you were a tourist and that we'd never see each other again.' She gazed at him with a hot mix of anger and guilt and sadness. It had been a fantasy experience, she'd not wanted to shatter its perfect illusion with morning-after awkwardness. 'It wasn't like you were planning a second date either. You were passing through.'

'So were you. Or so you led me to believe. You lied as much as I did that night.'

She shook her head. 'I *never* lied.'

He tensed. 'By omission, you definitely did.'

'What about everything you forgot to mention? Like, your real name. Your true intentions for being there. You never said you were looking for something to tear apart.'

'I'm not the one tearing apart valuable things. *You're* the one who's done that—keeping a child from his father.' His voice rose. 'There's no reason you can give that excuses your failure to tell me once you knew who I was.'

'*You* didn't want me to know who you really were. I only discovered that by accident months afterwards. But you were so comfortable to lie, which told me all I needed to know about your integrity.' She snapped at him. She didn't really mean it but emotion had overruled her tongue. 'I never would have said yes if I'd known who you were.'

'You would have said it faster,' he shot back.

'Oh, wow.' She drew in a shocked breath at his sheer arrogance. 'You think you're that amazing?'

He might be six feet three of muscled manly beauty, he might have a brilliant brain and he might have billions in the bank, but he had no integrity. And therefore, no true value.

'The resources I have are amazing.'

'You think I care about money?' she scoffed. She worked as a *volunteer*, the last thing she was interested in was accumulating material wealth. 'If I was a gold-digger, wouldn't I have beaten down your door the second I discovered who you really were?' She flushed angrily. 'I thought you were some chilled-out surfer. I had no reason to suspect you were a billionaire bulldozer who buys whatever he wants and then destroys it.'

'Destroys it?' His eyes widened. 'Are we talking about that dilapidated old hostel?'

'It wasn't dilapidated.'

'You showed me a prime piece of land that was in dire need of investment.'

She rejected that notion. Lucero's property had been perfect. Furthermore the old man had been unwaveringly kind to her. But now Javier was ripping apart his legacy. 'And didn't you take that information and use it well?' she raged. 'Well, you're not buying me and you're not buying my son.'

'He's my son too.' His eyes glittered, revealing his own loss of temper. 'It's eighteen months since that night, Emmy. And I've only just discovered he even *exists*. Now he's *nine* months old,' he said. 'I've missed out on almost the full first year of his life. That's unforgivable and you can't keep him from me. You owe me time.' He inhaled sharply and whirled away, clearly struggling to regain his self-control.

Emmy was struck still as her worst fears were realised. Javier was going to fight. He was used to getting his way. Was he going to do whatever it took to get it now? He had everything on his side—resources, power, privilege. She had only intuition and resolve and the fiercest love imaginable.

'Understand this,' she breathed. 'There's nothing I won't do to protect my son.' She would be there at every step. She would never let Javier or anyone else sideline her.

'Nothing? Good to know.' He turned back to face her. His lips curved in a smile full of *bring it on* challenge that fired up that dangerous part of Emerald. 'I consider myself warned. But somehow, I feel confident I can handle whatever you try to throw at me.' He stepped closer. 'You know I can handle you, Emerald.'

His words sent sparks cascading through her—anger, defiance, *attraction*. Unwanted, inappropriate, unstoppable attraction.

And she was furious about it.

CHAPTER TWO

'So, what do you want to do?'

Javier stared as Emerald Jones squared up to him.

Do? That was the terrible thing. Because the one thing that he wanted to do right now was the one thing he really, *really* shouldn't. This raw kick of lust was appalling. He decided it was anger, really, fuelling the hit of ill-timed appetite—his rage tempting him with one way in which he could assert control. Well, he wasn't going to let emotion get the better of him. Not *ever.* He very deliberately took a step back and shoved his hands into his pockets.

He'd come here today ready to apologise, ready to take on responsibility for his son, ready to support Emerald once they'd worked out how… But to discover she knew who he was already? And that she'd found him so lacking that she'd just 'not bothered' to let him know?

His gut clenched as he strove to think clearly and decide how best to answer her.

Frankly the last twenty-four hours were a blur. He'd engaged a private investigator to work urgently through the night the second he'd been driven away from the store yesterday. Javier had tossed and turned, recalculating, remembering, reliving. The confirmation had come mid-morning. Emerald Jones had delivered her son nine months ago and given him the name Lucero Ramon, Luke for short. Certainty had seared like a white-hot sword cauterising a stomach wound, leaving Javier so breathless he'd almost lost the power to think. He'd had to hurry paperwork to ensure visa requirements were met to get them both on board because he'd wanted to make sure they could have some time to talk—uninterrupted and safe. Although, truthfully, he had no idea where to start the conversation that was more than nine months overdue.

Now he steeled himself against her bone-weakening beauty. The linen shirt dress she wore today closely cupped her curves while the faded blue still brought out the blue of her emotion-laden eyes. But the accusation in them was laughably unjust when it turned out *she* was the one who'd hidden something far more serious. Her glorious hair hung in fiery, loose spirals halfway down her back and that reckless part of him wanted to tangle his fingers into them and pull her close. Instead he finally answered her question. 'Can you close the shop and get rid of that woman so we can talk—?'

'That's Connie,' Emerald interrupted shortly. 'She's amazing.'

'I'm sure, but we need some time alone.'

And he didn't really want to hear about the amazing Connie. Not when she was doing all the things he'd not even been given the chance to attempt—such as spending the afternoon with his son.

He had no real relationship with his own parents and frankly had no idea how to set about building one with a baby. He pushed back the slithering thought that it was too late already, that any relationship he might've fostered with Luke could never be recovered, that, once again, he'd missed out on something fundamental. He didn't have time to squander on that insecurity right now. And at the very least, he could give his son all outward signs of support.

But he couldn't stop himself from questioning her sharply. 'Were you *ever* going to tell me? Or were you hoping to get rid of me quickly and keep your secret? Were you going to deny me and *him* for ever?'

It wasn't the first time Javier had been betrayed, but it was absolutely the worst. An innocent child denied his birthright? How could she claim to love her son yet choose to deny him such a primary relationship? Would she deny him everything Javier *could* offer—his finance alone was outstanding and his son should never have to live in anything less than luxury. His tension coiled tighter with every second that she didn't reply.

'I don't know what I was going to do.'

'Well, we need to figure out things as quickly as possible,' he said, shoving the anger down inside so he could calmly take control of this mess. 'I'd like you to come with me—'

'I can't just walk out—'

'Sure you can,' he muttered in annoyance. 'You've done it before.'

She paled but argued anyway. 'I owe Connie. I need to give her proper notice.'

And she didn't owe *him*? Javier huffed out a tight breath. 'If she's that amazing, she'll understand how important this is.'

Emerald couldn't stall and deny him more time when he'd missed this much already.

'We need to go.' He rocked on his feet, resisting the urge to pace.

He could feel her aggression building, but she turned away. Stiffly she locked the store door and then led him up the narrow stairs to the tiny room above. A swift glance around the bedsit made him grit his teeth.

'Thanks, Connie,' Emerald said, her awkwardness evident in the colour storming her cheeks. 'I'm sorry, I had to close the shop.'

Javier didn't listen to the rest—their voices faded as he gazed in fascination, and frankly in trepidation, at the tiny boy playing on a mat on the floor. He was cherubic—there was no other word for it. A dumpling of a child with dark eyes, dark curls and a beatific smile. Javier felt something in his chest slip, but at the same time his gut tightened. He'd never felt as afraid for anything or anyone in his life. Nor had he felt as uncertain of what to actually do.

Moments later the older woman left. Javier didn't glance or give a damn about her obvious curiosity. He couldn't peel his attention from his son. He had little experience with children. He'd had no intention of having any of his own, but Luke was here and, now that he was, Javier couldn't have him denied his heritage or the opportunities he could offer. Which were a damn sight more than this sparse existence. He had to draw in another cooling breath to stop his temper from flaring again.

The child smiled at Emmy as she crouched and put a soft toy in front of him. Javier's gut twisted again as he watched her with Luke. Given the boy's gurgling gleeful reaction to her, it was obvious she'd cared for him but while he appreciated that, he was also...*jealous*? And there was something else—something worse—bubbling beneath his skin. Another scalding emotion that he didn't want to recognise, let alone release.

'Please start packing, Emerald,' he said bluntly.

She glanced up at him. He saw the nervous

lick of her lips. But it was the widening of the child's eyes that had him instantly regretting how harsh he'd sounded.

'It's not like I can steal him away without you knowing,' he added in a whisper. 'This room is ridiculously small.'

In an almost blinding wave of emotion, he realised he wanted his son to have *every-thing*. Not just material things, but emotional things—things Javier hadn't had. Security and consistency of care—for one. The trouble was, he didn't know how to begin with that. All he knew was that he needed to get them out of there.

Emerald stood, visibly drawing courage as she walked towards him. 'I thought we could have more of a conversation.'

'About what?' There was nothing to discuss. He could provide a better place for them, there was no question of that.

But as he watched the pulse at the side of her neck flutter, his own accelerated. And she still didn't begin to pack.

'I can't just leave,' she said.

'We need to work this out and we need time and space in which to do that.' He tried to stay reasonable. 'My place is bigger. Or do you want me to stay with you in this shoebox?' He couldn't resist stepping closer to her this time, or taking a Machiavellian delight in the way colour swarmed more boldly in her cheeks. 'Is that what you want? Me to share that narrow bed with you?'

Her lashes dropped, veiling a sudden flare in her eyes.

That other feeling ripped through him. The one he'd desperately wanted to ignore. The one he'd given way to with such glee all those months ago. He gritted his teeth and cursed himself.

This woman had kept the most precious thing from him and when she'd discovered the truth of who he was, she'd still denied him, yet still all his body wanted was to haul hers beneath his so he could sample her sweet fervour. She'd been so hot that night and he ached to seduce her into that soft, arching slickness once more. He loathed his own weakness.

'I can't spend another night apart from him, Emmy,' he said harshly, curling his hands into fists in his pockets to stop himself from reaching for her and admitting a painful truth in the process. 'I have too much to catch up on.'

'You can't stay here,' she said.

'Then you'd better start packing.' He paced away from her, turning to watch the boy from the safety of the window.

'Where are you staying?' she asked dully.

He didn't feel like answering. He didn't want to waste time or energy on words when the answer would be obvious soon enough. He had too much to process already. Moodily he watched his son. He had no idea how to even approach him.

'Javier.'

He glanced over at the hesitation in her voice.

'Will we be returning here?' Her blue eyes were very wide, very worried.

He steeled himself against the emotion and the effect it had deep inside him. 'What do you think?'

She blinked rapidly. 'You can't just expect us both to move in with you.' She squared her shoulders. 'I have a position here in which Luke can be with me full time. It's the perfect arrangement.'

'Perfect?' He almost choked. 'Living in this

tiny room above a store where he's exposed to exhaust fumes and strangers coming in and out all the time? You're busy—he could get into strife when your back is turned.'

She stiffened. 'I would never allow that to happen—'

'But it could.' He was laying it on thick, but he needed to win and he was going with his strongest play—which was her obvious desire to protect her son. 'It's not perfect for *him*. Or *me*.'

She swallowed. 'You expect me to give up everything?'

'You did that to me.' As he gazed at her, the anger and desire within him coalesced. 'So for eighteen months, yeah. You give up everything.' The thought of having her with him, within his power, was appallingly appealing and he couldn't resist demanding it. After all, wasn't it only right and fair?

Not fair. His conscience needled, but the anger drowned out the discord.

'Eighteen months?' Her jaw dropped. 'Luke's only nine months old.'

'I missed every moment of your pregnancy.'

'That wasn't your—that was my...' She trailed off at the look in his eyes.

Eighteen months. Now he'd said it, he'd settle for nothing less.

'I think if you tell Connie the truth, she'll understand completely,' he said crisply. 'I'm sure she'll be pleased to see you both in a better situation and for Luke to have his father in his life.'

He'd never wanted a family on terms like this—a surprise with a woman he barely knew and who'd hidden the truth from him. But he'd do what was right by his son. He'd do better than his own parents had done for him. Somehow. He was determined to.

'How long have you known?' Emerald asked as she fetched a worn striped bag and opened it up. 'Javier?' she prompted when he didn't respond.

He clenched his jaw but knew he had to make an effort and respond even though he hated reliving that moment he'd seen her again. 'I saw you from a distance yesterday afternoon when Connie was returning Luke to you. If I hadn't been there...' That possibility made him see red again. 'So it's only a few hours since I saw his birth certificate.' He broke off, determined to control his surge of anger, purely because of the small piece of innocence cooing on the play mat. 'He deserves the best from both of us.'

Emmy stared at Javier. The remnants of anger and hurt were evident in his eyes but she also saw that, despite his reluctance to speak more, he was trying. And what choice did she have? He was *right*. Luke deserved better and she had failed him. She'd been too scared to reach out once she knew who her 'Ramon' really was.

But the feeling she was fighting hardest? That slithering ripple of desire that had twisted into life the second she'd seen him again. And the moment he'd mentioned sleeping in her small bed? A wave of heat engulfed her again. It was so wrong. So stupid and selfish and wrong.

'It won't take me long to pack.' Her voice cracked and she hurriedly began filling her bag. She didn't have much, nor did Luke, so it wouldn't take long. But as she shoved their belongings together, she couldn't let this continue without trying to explain herself a little more to Javier.

'I left early that morning because I had to get

to a project on another island. I've been a volunteer abroad for a while,' she said. 'That night, I'd just wanted an escape and you were...' She trailed off and swallowed uncomfortably. She couldn't explain that bit any more—it was too embarrassing to admit how she'd decided to keep that night as the fantasy it had been. She'd not wanted to spoil the memory of it with an awkward goodbye that next morning.

'When I realised I was pregnant I was worried,' she continued as Javier stood still as still by the window, silently watching. 'I hid it for as long as I could because I couldn't afford to lose my volunteer visa. But then Lucero, the head of the foundation, found out. He was very kind. He helped me, so did others in the community.' She had been so grateful to the elderly man when she'd had nowhere else to go. 'I didn't discover *your* real identity until the property deal was announced after he died. Luke was already a few months old.'

That time had been horrible. She'd been alone, angry, scared, so tired and so broke she was trapped. She'd been grateful and dependent on first Lucero's, then Connie's support. And when she'd finally found out who Javier really was, she'd become terrified that he might find out about their baby. 'I felt betrayed. Lucero was gone, you'd lied. I was hormonal and I had this tiny little boy who'd become the most precious thing in my life and when I learned who you really were I was afraid...' She trailed off again and shook her head hopelessly. How could she ever explain herself to Javier without telling him the rest of her background? But it was too dangerous to do that. She couldn't trust he wouldn't use it against her.

'Afraid of what?' Javier eventually prompted.

She shrugged. 'That you'd swoop in and take him from me.'

She registered the immediate flash of furious hurt in his eyes.

Maybe he'd think she was irrational or over-emotional or something. But the fear of him taking Luke from her *wasn't* irrational in her view. Because that was what happened. Powerful people took away the things she loved most. Powerful people judged and they'd always found her wanting. People had judged her all her life—slandering her intentions and decisions. Because of her parents, her brother and, yes, the mistakes she'd made herself. People who knew her past didn't trust her. So she didn't trust people in return. Particularly if they had privilege and money and Javier Torres had both.

She had no power with which to fight him, so she'd felt she had no choice but to hide. Luke was too precious. And how could she trust Javier when he'd lied to her from the first?

There was another long moment of silence and she sensed him grappling the emotion, almost as if he were carefully choosing what words he was comfortable to release.

'I'm not a *monster*, Emerald. But make no mistake, I'm no hero either,' he said so expressionlessly that she shivered. 'So I'm swooping in and taking you too.'

His expression was now so fixed it was unreadable—and he was so far from the smiling man she'd met on the beach that evening.

'Is that everything packed?' he asked curtly.

Didn't he want to hear more of her side of the story? Didn't he want to ask more or offer any further explanation of his own actions? Didn't he want to forgive her?

No. Of course he didn't. People who were quick to judge never did. They didn't want to revise their opinions once they'd leapt to their conclusions.

She felt sick. She'd been lost in a fog of desperation, struggling to feed Luke and scared for their future—afraid that exactly *this* would happen. She couldn't risk telling Javier all her truth now, not when he was this remote and disapproving. Her whole background would appal him. But this time she couldn't pack her bag and run away. She had to stay and fight for Luke. She'd escaped her past before, she'd figure out a way to get through this too. And nothing mattered more than Luke's well-being. She'd put up with anything to ensure he was safe and well.

But she wondered if Javier could say the same. Or was this just a powerful man used to being in control venting his anger at being kept in the dark? Was this about him getting control back more than it was about Luke?

'You don't want children,' she said before thinking better of it. 'You couldn't have made it clearer. That night you even said you weren't interested in marriage and kids.'

'Of course I made that clear,' he said frozenly from his spot by the window. 'I always do that to put off women who might think having my baby would set them up for life.' He shot her a pointed look. 'And I needed to be extra clear with an inexperienced woman who'd neglected to mention that she was a virgin until the very moment we were about to have sex. I had to ensure she wasn't hearing wedding bells.'

Her jaw dropped at his outrageous arrogance. 'You think you're some hot catch? No woman who knows what you're really like would *ever* want to marry you.'

His shoulders lifted and dropped dismissively. 'It's amazing what people will put up with when there's a hefty bank balance on offer.'

'Well, it ought to be obvious now that I don't want your money.' She flushed. 'Nor do I want *you.*'

There was such guarded coolness in those cocoa and coffee eyes. 'Legally Luke will be my son and heir,' he countered quietly. 'We don't need to marry to give him my name. That's a simple certificate change.'

'What about my name?' she asked nervously. 'He has that now.'

'No reason why he can't have mine too.

Jones-Torres or Torres-Jones.' He shrugged. 'We can flip a coin later.'

So there was to be none of that *you must marry me now* old-fashioned autocratic drama? He was making out as if this were easy. Emotionless.

But it wasn't. Misery swamped her as Javier asserted his paternal authority. But didn't he have every right to do that? She owed. And his calm, apparent reasonableness made her feel worse for having kept quiet these last two months. So now she faced eighteen months of living with him and then what—some shared care arrangement, with Javier offering their son a lifestyle that she could *never* equal or compete with? She almost bent double with despair at the prospect. She'd inevitably be shut out of Luke's life.

'I'll carry the bag, you take Luke,' he said stiffly. 'It might take us a little time to get acquainted.'

Downstairs Connie sent her an anxious look as Javier carried her bags to the big black SUV waiting outside.

'He's Luke's father, isn't he?' Connie swiftly whispered as soon as he was out of earshot.

'It's that obvious?' Emmy asked.

'You don't talk with any man, ever.' Connie smiled. 'And then you bring him upstairs when you're supposed to be working?'

It wasn't as if she'd had much choice. 'Back then, I didn't know who he was...' Her voice faded and she swallowed through the sudden tightness.

'Are you okay?' Connie stepped closer.

Emmy's heart broke at that concern but she quickly nodded, not wanting to get emotional. 'I will be. We will be.'

'Stay in touch. Please let me know how you are...' Connie gave Emmy's arm a gentle squeeze and pressed a quick kiss on Luke's head. 'I'm going to miss you both.'

'I'm going to miss you too.' Emmy's breath caught and she blinked back sudden tears. 'Thank you so much for everything. We couldn't have survived without you.'

Connie's grip on her arm tightened. 'You're a survivor, don't forget that.'

Her support gave Emmy a much-needed boost. She *was* a survivor and she loved Luke as no one else in the world could. But then she saw the car seat already fixed in the rear of the car and reality hit again. Javier had arrived with no intention of leaving *without* their son. What else did he have planned that she didn't know about yet?

'Are you staying at a hotel?' she asked nervously as she sat in the back between Javier and Luke. 'Which one?'

Javier didn't reply as the driver pulled away from the store. Emmy didn't push it. He clearly valued privacy for personal conversations, and that was fair enough.

Less than fifteen minutes later they pulled up, not at a hotel, but rather the marina. Emmy's heart took a knock as she saw a sleek speedboat idling at the dock. A crewman stepped forward when he saw the car pull in.

Emerald put her hand over Luke's tiny one and he gripped her finger. She had no family. Nowhere to go. No one to turn to. Connie was old and had limited resources, she'd helped her the best she could and Emmy couldn't take advantage of her generosity any longer. She had to deal with this alone.

'I don't think that boat is safe for Luke,' she said, desperately searching for a reason to refuse to board.

Javier glanced at her coolly. 'Do you think I would endanger him?' he asked softly.

The tiny hairs rose on the back of Emmy's neck. 'Of course not.'

'Good. We're staying on my yacht.'

Emmy tensed, trying not to let her reaction show because that didn't feel safe for *her*. On a yacht, they'd be isolated and too...*close*. She'd be vulnerable—not because she was physically *afraid* of him, but because she was attracted to him still. She had the feeling he could emotionally devastate her on more than one level and on some small yacht, there'd be no escape.

Javier took the tiny life jacket the waiting crewman now held out for them and turned to where she stood holding their baby. 'This is only for the speedboat. The yacht has been baby-proofed.'

Emmy gritted her teeth and put the jacket on her son; she'd wait and see this yacht for herself to decide what was safe for him.

'I have one for you too,' Javier added.

She glared at him. 'I can swim.'

Javier stared back at her. 'Put it on or I'll put it on for you.'

For a long moment they clashed in silence—

the storm of emotion slowly changed the colour of Javier's eyes from that cocoa mix to almost all pure black coffee and Emmy suddenly found herself relenting. 'Will you hold him while I put mine on, then?' she half choked.

To her surprise, Javier's eyes widened uneasily, but he didn't hesitate to reply. 'Of course.'

He held his hands out awkwardly and Emmy placed her son into them.

As Emmy swiftly shrugged the jacket on, Luke contemplated Javier seriously while Javier gazed back at Luke—the wary curiosity in their expressions was identical.

'I can take him now.' Emmy held her hands out the second she was done with her jacket.

Luke babbled at Javier in that exact moment.

'No, that's okay,' Javier said brusquely. 'I've got him.'

A hot wash of discomfort flooded her as she followed them to the speedboat. Was she jealous? Or worse, were her ovaries exploding all over again at the sight of her son and his father assessing each other with such fascination?

The crewman had already stowed her bag, so within two minutes they were moving. The speedboat chugged slower than she suspected it usually did. It was then that she finally paid attention and realised to which vessel they were heading. It had been half hidden beyond a small tour vessel and it wasn't a yacht at all. It was a floating *mansion*. It gleamed as if new—its navy and white trim stylish and the chrome fittings almost blinding in the sun. As they came right alongside she stared, counting the levels up. There were at least four decks she could see. Was there a bunch of other passengers already on there?

'Is this yours?' she asked as she climbed aboard, her arms feeling empty as he still carried Luke.

'You don't like it?'

No one could *not* like it, but Emmy had never felt as uncomfortable in all her life. Was he really this wealthy? 'It's…massive. I thought you were all about environmental eco-tourism.'

'In this instance,' he clipped, 'I'm all about privacy.'

Not even the luxury cruise boats she'd seen arriving here had this detail and comfort. The wooden decks gleamed while the soft furnishings were rich and lavish. There was obviously no expense spared, every fitting and comfort designer. It's opulence and extravagance were staggering.

'Where will Luke and I be staying?'

To her relief he passed Luke back to her. 'Follow me.'

It was going to take her days to find her way around this floating palace. She was hopelessly confused as she followed him up another flight of gleaming steps and along an extraordinarily wide corridor.

'This is your suite,' he said briskly. 'A cabin for Luke has been prepared right next door.'

Emmy barely glanced into her space, but Luke's stunned her. It was huge, with gorgeous curtains dressing the wide windows offering stunning views across the water. There was a cot set up already dressed in beautiful white linen. A mobile hung above it while other baby supplies were stacked neatly in the corner.

Once again the detailed preparation stretched her nerves. What did he want, really?

'You got this ready quickly.' She stepped back out to the corridor, almost bumping into Javier and flushing hotly at the near miss. 'Where's your room?'

'I'm on the deck above.'

Javier sleeping on another level was reassuring, wasn't it? Yet she had a sharp twinge of disappointment. She shook herself and forced her focus onto her little boy. She couldn't believe the size of the cabins or that there could be this much space on a private yacht. She'd be sure to keep both her and Luke's doors open through the night, because she'd never slept in a different room from her son. She tightened her hold on him without thinking and, at the change, Luke wriggled and began to fret.

'He's tired and hungry.' She glanced at Javier defensively.

'I suspect he might not be the only one.' The faintest smile flashed on Javier's face. 'So let's get you both fed.'

Emmy's irritation bloomed. She was *not* some overtired, hungry toddler. 'No, I'd like to unpack his things first.'

Javier drew an audible breath. 'Fine.'

But to her chagrin, Javier didn't leave, rather he went right into Luke's cabin and sat down in the wide armchair.

'Will you hold him while I do it?' she asked.

Again there was that wariness in Javier's

eyes, but he answered coolly enough. 'Of course.'

She handed Luke back to Javier, quickly finding Luke's favourite toy so he could clutch it while she swiftly emptied the bag she'd packed.

Javier sat carefully holding Luke while intently watching her unload every item. 'All these things are Luke's. Where are your things?'

'Still in the bag. I'll unload the rest in my room later.'

'That bag is nearly empty.'

She shrugged. 'I don't need much.'

'You spend everything you have on him,' Javier said flatly.

'Of course.' She flushed and concentrated on refolding Luke's few clothes.

'He's bottle-fed?' he asked after a moment.

She swallowed hard, feeling her defensiveness flare again. Was he going to criticise all her choices? 'He's starting solid foods now. I breastfed for as long as I could—'

'I'm not judging,' Javier said calmly. 'I'm just understanding the process. If he takes a bottle, then it doesn't need to be you who feeds him.

I could do that.' He looked at her. 'You don't think I'd want to feed my own child? Know how to soothe him when he's unwell or un-happy?'

She stared at him. Did he really mean that? Did he want to be that involved? Stupidly the thought terrified her more.

'Does he wake through the night?' Javier asked.

'Sometimes.' She didn't want to admit how demanding Luke could be, but the fact was he was a strong little boy with a healthy appetite and his curious mind was developing rapidly too, which meant he craved more stimulation.

'A nanny could manage him for that.'

'A nanny?' Emmy stiffened. 'I don't need a nanny.'

'You need some help. We both do.'

'I haven't up until this point.' Her hackles lifted instantly as she feared this was the first step towards eliminating her.

'Are you sure you want to argue this now, Emmy?' he asked softly.

But a torrent of bitterness was rising within her. If he wanted to employ a nanny, then he didn't really want to care for his son himself.

So did he regard his son simply as an acquisition? Fears coalesced, sending her into a heightened state of confusion and defensiveness, and she lashed out. 'This isn't actually about Luke, is it? This is about you not being in control before. You not knowing he existed. You can't stand that.'

Javier's expression shuttered. 'This is utterly and only about Luke and what's best for him.'

'And you think a nanny is best? Not his own parents?'

Something flickered in his eyes before he blinked it away. 'I think his parents are important. *Both* of them.' He gazed down at Luke's head.

He said that with such fierce conviction Emmy wondered at it, but before she could ask why he felt that so strongly, he lifted his head and fixed her in place with that ruthlessly assessing stare of his.

'But we need to be in the best frame of mind to be the best we can for him,' he added. 'Right now you need food and rest as much as he does. Come on.' He hefted their small son in his arms and stood. 'We'll eat in the dining room.'

He exited the cabin so swiftly Emmy was left staring agape. Seriously? Was he just going to walk away from her concerns? From this conversation?

Her irritation brewing, she ran after him. The stunning superyacht stole her breath but at the same time stoked her anger. It was ludicrously indulgent. The gleaming marble, backlit gemstones, the polished silverware, the plush sofas and soft cushions and above all sheer size and *space*. Everything was so ornate and over the top it screamed obscene wealth. Even the discretion of the uniformed crew irritated her. They disappeared before she barely caught a glimpse of them—obviously well trained, well paid, well controlled. Had he led her to this formal dining room to intimidate her—to make her painfully aware of everything he had to offer and everything she didn't? There was even a highchair for Luke already. Discomfort and fury mounting, she settled him into it and fastened the small belt.

'I wasn't sure of your tastes, or what time we'd get here, so I requested a small buffet,' Javier said smoothly, preventing her from saying anything more again with sudden 'top host' manners. 'Help yourself.'

She couldn't bring herself to put anything on her plate despite the sudden watering of her mouth at the sumptuous array of freshly prepared, beautiful food. It had been a long time since she'd had anything more than a quick thrown-together comfort eat, but she selected some mashed plantain to put on Luke's tray.

'Stop the stiff-necked pride,' he said, taking the seat next to the one she'd perched on and dispensing with the manners all over again. 'Or I'll feed you myself.'

'I'm not very hungry,' she lied and instantly hated herself for it. Since when was she so shrewish? But as she glanced around the room again, more of the same leaked out. 'You don't scare me with your display of wealth.'

'Emmy.' He calmly served himself a portion of fresh-cooked fish and fragrant rice. 'We're in this room purely for the privacy. I don't want the world staring at us if we're up on deck.'

Her pulse settled fractionally, but she was still tense. Luke, on the other hand, was delightedly experimenting with the snippets of food she'd put in front of him.

Javier was watching Luke with such naked fascination that Emmy felt badly about her exhausted, emotion-clouded judgement of only seconds ago. She wanted to smooth this awkwardness somehow, but before she could speak her stomach rumbled embarrassingly loudly. Javier's eyebrows lifted and his mouth quirked. She shelved her pride and served herself. She almost moaned at her first bite of the seafood. She hadn't had anything as delicious in a long while.

She saw Javier's smile broaden and decided to let him have the win. She did feel better.

'We need to talk—' she finally began, breaking off when she saw him grimace.

'We need time,' he replied after a moment. 'Eighteen months is a good start. We'll work out a permanent arrangement eventually, but by then Luke will likely be ready to spend time mixing with other children in a good preschool.'

'You want to send him to school already?' She gaped at him.

Javier paused. 'Part-time play with other children might be good. I don't want him to be lonely.'

Meaning Javier wasn't about to have any other children? Given that Emmy wasn't either, it shouldn't have mattered, but his pronouncement bothered her all the same. And this wasn't her idea of a conversation, this was him just deciding. She chewed, swallowed and stabbed another forkful of suddenly tasteless food. Her control wasn't just slipping, it was being torn from her. No decisions about Luke would be only hers again. That realisation both discomforted her and made her feel guilty all over again because it gave her the smallest insight into how Javier must feel about missing out on everything so far.

'Okay.' She nodded.

But the problem was she didn't want to live with Javier. She could hardly bear to be this close to him. It was unsettling in ways she didn't want to define, and she definitely didn't want to *take* anything from him. At the same time she couldn't deny him what he needed— that she did owe—time with Luke. And she was too selfish to give up any time with her son herself. So she had to stay.

'You'll need more than what you've brought on board,' he murmured.

'No, I won't.' She tried to stay calm.

'You're living under my roof, at my insistence. I'll take care of your expenses while you're here.'

She shook her head.

'You'll definitely need warmer clothes for winter in New York.'

She was hardly going to be out and about in the city. She'd be with Luke. 'I'll figure something out.' She had almost zero savings, but she was going to have to make them stretch. And she definitely needed to think about how she could support herself in the future. She was used to living a roving existence— volunteering on various projects for lodging and food as she explored the world. Even with Luke with her, she'd thought she might be able to make it work when he was a little older. But no more. She'd be bound to wherever Javier wanted Luke—and by extension her—to be. 'I don't need anything from you.'

Javier was watching her closely. 'It doesn't bother me.'

Was that a flicker of amusement in his eyes?

'It bothers me.' She still heard the echo of the insults and insinuations through her pregnancy when a couple of people had whispered about her relationship with the elderly Lucero.

Not to mention Javier's own implied insults when he'd 'explained' why he'd not given her his real name and his arrogant assumption that women wanted a wedding band when they knew who he really was.

While other people might've been able to laugh those things off, she couldn't, because she'd come from a family with no moral boundaries, who wanted nothing more than a free ride at someone else's expense. She never wanted to be anything like them and she'd spent most of her life trying to prove she wasn't.

'I get that you want to provide for our son, that's wonderful,' she said in a low voice. 'But *I* will not touch a cent of your money. I don't want it and I don't need it.'

Javier leaned back in the seat and actually grinned at her. 'Fine. I'll pay you as his carer, then.'

'That's not acceptable to me.' She couldn't even look at him now he was smiling. 'I don't want your money.'

'Well it'll be there,' he replied carelessly. 'It's up to you whether you use it or not.'

That glimpse of good humour recharged the cells of attraction she'd been trying to suppress. He was far too gorgeous and far too close for comfort and this sudden return to affable and easy-going was alarming. Maybe it was wrong of her, but she still couldn't trust him. She couldn't trust anyone. But most of all, she suddenly realised, she couldn't trust *herself*. Because when he smiled at her like that? She was so tempted to lean in and smile back.

Suddenly she actually *appreciated* the size of the superyacht. It was big enough for them to avoid each other. She could have her time with Luke and he could have his.

And that, she realised, was the only way she was going to survive this.

Almost two hours later Javier watched Emmy needlessly adjust the light blanket covering their small son. Luke was fast asleep now, having listened to a story cradled in her arms before she put him into the cot.

'Come on,' he commanded her softly. 'We need to talk.'

It was the last thing he wanted to do. The tension he'd been containing for hours bubbled, seeping out of the lid he'd had shoved on it all day. He knew she'd been scraping an existence as a volunteer for a long time, living above that store, effectively working for free. And now, despite that dinner, she still looked pale and exhausted and terrified. It annoyed him immensely. What was it about him that scared her so? He wanted that fiery woman he'd met on the beach back. Memory surged—she'd looked so liberated and confident and they'd had fun together. More than fun. He remembered the look in her eyes, the sighs she'd released. He *knew* she'd had pleasure with him. And yes, his body tensed, any desire for *conversation* evaporated completely.

'Sit down before you fall down, Emmy,' he growled, mad with himself for remembering the heat of her response. 'And relax.'

'Relax?' She threw him a stunned look as she sank onto the cushions. 'How can I when everything is happening so fast?' She buried her face in her hands. He saw her short-bitten nails, the blister on her knuckle and the tiredness in her slumped shoulders.

Inwardly he cursed again that she'd not contacted him. It was beyond insulting, but it had also hurt *her*. She'd clearly almost been broken trying to survive, despite the little help she'd accepted from those few people. And why had she needed the help of them? Where was her family? She'd said she'd travelled a lot, before stopping here because of Luke, so why had she named her son for an elderly man she'd only known a couple of years?

'Look, just breathe,' he muttered. 'We'll take this one day at a time.'

Her determined independence infuriated him, but he'd overcome it. Oddly he wanted her to feel safe enough to let him take some of the load she'd denied him all these months. And he wanted—

'Why did you lie?' She lifted her head and challenged him again. 'I've tried to explain my actions but you've said almost nothing about yours—offered no *real* reason for why you didn't even tell me your name. Did you want anonymity? To escape the pressure of being a billionaire? Did you just want an ordinary moment with no one watching so you could seduce some stranger without any repercussions?' She shook her head. 'Sorry about that, Javier. But maybe you should try some time on Struggle Street or what it's like to be judged the second someone learns your name.'

He blinked, taken aback by her sudden ferocity. His defences instinctively rose because these kinds of questions were not ones he ever answered. 'You've no idea what I've been through, Emmy,' he muttered in an instinctive unthinking response. 'None of the struggles I've faced.'

'Enlighten me, then,' she dared with a mutinous lift to her chin. 'Tell me something meaningful. Because we have to work through this. We have a child together and we're going to need to get to know each other.'

No, they didn't. He glared at her, rejecting that idea completely. He and Emerald were Luke's parents, yes. They didn't need to be anything more to each other. They didn't need to 'open up' and reveal all. They only needed to be able to work together.

He saw the blaze in her eyes ignite and struggled to hold back his urge to respond in a far too physical fashion. Yes, the real problem here was he was only interested in getting to know *her* in that one, most carnal way all over again. 'Not tonight.' He gritted his teeth and shut her down, holding back everything else he wanted to *do*.

She was clearly exhausted and beyond the fire, in the shining depths of her blue eyes, he could see a soft entreaty—the desire for something he couldn't offer anyone. She sought emotional intimacy—as if he could build a relationship? *No, thank you, and never.*

'Javier?' she prompted, her temper sparking.

He didn't blame her for getting angry. But he could hardly admit that now he had her alone, and with time on his side, the last thing he wanted to do was talk. He strove to resist the urge to pull her against him, to remind her that they already knew all they needed to make each other feel physically fantastic. 'We have eighteen months to discover whatever we actually need to know,' he growled dismissively. 'Right now I think it's best if you get some rest.'

Her jaw dropped. 'Are you sending me to bed?'

He couldn't tell if the provocation in her eyes and luscious pout was deliberate or not. But it was too powerful for him to stand. He stared at her for a long moment, his inner tension stringing him out.

'No, that's up to you,' he growled, mentally pleading with his hormones for mercy before rising and walking away. 'But *I* need some time out.'

CHAPTER THREE

'HEY.'

'Hey, yourself.'

Cool waves washed over Emmy's feet as she watched the tall hunk of stranger stroll across the white sands towards her as if he'd just walked off the set of an old-school Hepburn movie. He had sandals on and faded red swim shorts finished halfway down muscled thighs—but other than that, he was bare. The waistband of his shorts rode low and a little askew, revealing acres of bronzed skin, smoothly stretched over ridged abs and a wide, well-defined masculine chest. His shoulders were broad and strong. After a couple of moments she had to consciously close her mouth so she wasn't just standing there gaping at him, but it was almost impossible to believe he was real.

She blinked, pleased to discover he was still there. Still smiling. Still walking towards her. As he neared, she saw his face in greater detail—chiselled jaw, lips curved in an open smile—but it was the deep, dark brown eyes that ensnared her—cocoa-ringed black coffee, two of her favourite things and they were impossible to turn away from. She'd encountered a bunch of handsome tourists in her few months on the Galapagos so far, but none like this guy. And it wasn't his jaw-dropping handsome features—each one alone enough to melt any woman—it was the confident, casual manner with which he moved. He had an aura of easy assurance together with an indefinable quality that commanded attention even here, in one of the most untamed, unique places in the world where there were mind-blowing wonders to see in every direction.

Emmy grew conscious of her green bikini—not that it was skimpy, but it hardly hid her curves. Sadly her kaftan was further up the sand in a heap of worn silk, beneath the watchful gaze of one of the many resting sea lions. She'd spent the day combing the beaches for any small pieces of plastic as part of her volunteer placement with the Flores Foundation and had come to the water to cool off and have some quiet time.

'You might want to watch out for my friend there.' She jerked her head towards the nearby sea lion as the man set down the old rucksack he'd had slung over one shoulder. An ancient wetsuit sleeve poked out of the broken zipper opening.

'He's possessive?' The handsome man cast a curious glance at the creature.

'And he has a few friends a few more feet away.'

He nodded and turned back to her with a smile. 'Amazing, isn't it? An incredible beach with beautiful, wild things everywhere.'

'Yes.' But she shied away from the glint of intimacy and double meaning in his eyes. 'There's so much beauty, it's hard to know where to look.'

'Oh, I know exactly where to look.' He watched her intently.

She couldn't break away from his gaze and as she watched, a wicked smile backlit his eyes.

'I've been admiring the boobies,' he added softly.

She rolled her eyes, but he'd said it so lightly,

with such a disarming smile, that it didn't sound either sleazy or cheesy when rightfully it ought to have been both. *'Really.'*

'You know, the bluer the feet, the more attractive the bird,' he added conversationally, as if he'd been talking about the birds all along.

The red- and blue-footed boobies were unique to the Galapagos—some curious, some ambivalent, all fascinating.

'And you know it's the males who need to woo their mate,' she said. *'They're* the ones who have to look good and do all the hard work.'

His grin widened to one of pure appreciation. 'Dance well? Strut hard and puff out their chests?'

'Generally look ridiculous, yes.'

'Ridiculous?' He pressed his hand to his very fine chest. 'Ouch.' Laughter crinkled the corners of his eyes.

His smile was the sort that stole hearts at first glance. Her pulse, already thready, sped faster. 'You shouldn't be here, you know.'

'It's private?'

'It's late,' she corrected. 'You might get lost trying to find your way back.'

'Is there a dragon who appears at dusk, to protect its fair maiden?'

Fair maiden? *Really?* She bit back a laugh. 'Perhaps I'm the dragon. My hair only hints at my fire.'

'That I can believe.' He slowly smiled again. 'Yet it doesn't scare you off?'

'Oh, no,' he said breezily. 'I'm not afraid of getting burned.'

She laughed out loud at that. 'Perhaps you should be. You shouldn't be scarred.'

His eyebrows danced upwards. 'Maybe my skin is thick and impenetrable and thus does a very good job of protecting my vital organs.'

'Such as your heart?' She nodded with another little laugh, so not surprised by that idea. 'So if you're so well armoured, then your prey must surely be at greater risk.'

'Risk? From me?' He smiled but there was seriousness in his eyes and he slowly shook his head. 'Dragons are rare and potentially vulnerable, and I don't think beautiful wild creatures should be either tamed or slain. Ideally they're not hurt in any way. I think they should be admired and appreciated and allowed to remain free.'

Of course he did—how safe for him. She suspected he was the wildest of all the beautiful creatures—not *her* at all. But she chuckled at the weak flirtation.

'What's your name?' he asked.

'Emerald.'

'Green?' He frowned slightly. 'You could be Sapphire, for your eyes.'

'I think my parents hoped my eyes might darken that way...'

'But you did your own thing?'

'Always.' It was a bit of bravado, because she hadn't always. But she did now. She'd learned well. Independence was everything. But perhaps, not isolation—not all the time. Not when she was confronted with a temptation like no other. Her heart thudded faster as he smiled.

'You could be Ruby for your hair, Pearl for your smile or Goldie for your skin—'

'Oh, no.' She rolled her eyes at the ridiculousness. 'That's too much of a leap. You can't get past these...' She pointed at the freckles on her arm, an example of the speckles that covered her all over.

'They're beautiful.' He shrugged lightly. 'The sun has kissed where I want to.'

Her jaw dropped that time. 'They're everywhere.'

'Precisely.'

'Oh.' She flushed awkwardly. 'Smooth.'

He laughed, a light teasing dare. 'You're such a treasure, I think I should call you *preciosa*.'

'Sure. You can do that.' She rolled her eyes.

His Spanish flowed and she suspected he was perfectly bilingual, in fact he probably spoke other languages too. He had an air of complete capability—as if he'd be a champion surfer as well, a super-achiever in all areas of life.

'And what should I call you?' she asked.

'Ramon.' There'd been the slightest hesitation before he replied. 'Why are you here?' he asked. 'All alone and looking like you just emerged from the sea like some mythical creature destined to destroy the heart of some poor hapless man?'

'I already told you.' She smiled. 'I'm waiting for the moon to complete my transformation into a dragon. And you're hardly hapless—you have that flame-proof skin, right?'

'So I've always thought.' His gaze dipped before flicking back up to her face.

That frisson travelled along her wiring, electrifying her circuitry. She saw the flash of recognition in his cocoa and coffee eyes. It didn't matter what they were saying—the weak innuendo and frothy banter was amusing but ultimately meaningless. Because it was already there, that connection forged between them at first glance. Absolute and instant attraction, translating to heat and want. And Emmy— who'd never encouraged even the slightest of flirtations, who'd never actually felt the desire to before—found herself sliding at speed into the ultimate temptation. For the first time, she reached for a moment she truly wanted, a moment with a man for herself.

'Shall I show you something even more beautiful?' she asked huskily.

His eyes widened. 'Yes, please.'

The bay was stunningly private. A colourful Sally Lightfoot crab scuttled and under the watchful gaze of wildlife unafraid of human contact, she trod a path known only to a few. Emmy didn't trust other people the way these animals did. It was only a short walk to another, smaller bay even more private than the first. It was rarely visited; people didn't get past that other one, thinking they'd made it to paradise already. But it was here, hidden and safe. Set back from the sand was an old wooden boat shed that belonged to her boss, Lucero Flores. It was his private place, set on the very edge of his holdings.

'This is incredible,' Ramon muttered as he reached out to take her hand as naturally and easily as breathing.

Emmy's pulse stumbled.

It was a stunning, magical secret but for the first time she was happy to share it. 'Isn't it?'

Time stretched as they walked the length of the beach and explored the shed—laughingly dodging the wildlife unafraid to make it their home already. And somehow that invisible connection pulled them together. A languorous heat invaded her limbs, slowing her movements as he closed the last gap to brush his lips across hers. That frisson of electricity skated down her spine and radiated along her limbs.

'Ramon,' she breathed. 'Ramon.'

It was the oddest, most delicious thing. She was melting, while at the same time energy coiled deep within. With a sigh she let it release, lost in sensations she'd not known she was capable of. All she knew was that she wanted more.

Emmy woke with a start, the soft cotton sheets tangled around her and her own voice echoing in her head. The dream wasn't a dream, it was a *memory*—every word real and she was burning as hot as the moment it had actually happened. Horrified, she clutched the sheet and sat up—she'd been moaning his name!

Or at least, his *other* name.

She gazed at the open door where light gleamed and quickly scrambled from the bed. She was utterly mortified, hoping she hadn't woken her son. Or that anyone *else* had heard her. She ran along the corridor and into Luke's room but froze on the threshold. The sheets were pulled back to reveal his empty cot.

Panic hit like a bucket of iced water. She froze where seconds ago she'd been searing. She hurriedly returned to her room, pulled on her dress. With a push of a button the heavy curtains slid back from the large windows. She stared out in horror. The marina was missing.

There was only the vast blue of the pristine Pacific Ocean. They were no longer off the coast of Santa Cruz. In fact, now she'd stopped to think, she realised the yacht was actually moving and she had no idea where they were. Or where Luke was. Not stopping to drag a comb through her curls, she sprinted upstairs, cursing the size of the yacht and all the confusing levels.

'Javier?' she called as she finally found the dining deck. 'Where—?' She broke off, startled to see two suited men seated at the table with a far too relaxed-looking Javier.

Who were they? When had they arrived? Where was Luke?

'Ah, Emmy.' Javier stood before she could ask any of the billion questions flooding her head. 'Come through, Luke will be excited to see you.' He sheltered her from the eyes of those two men. 'He's just through here.'

'You left him alone?' Emmy whispered as she followed him down another corridor.

'Of course not.'

A few feet from the open doorway she could see Luke safely ensconced on a play mat with one of the crew. 'Why didn't you wake me?'

'You were fast asleep, I didn't want to disturb you.'

Emmy froze. He'd seen her sleeping? Fragments of that dream—that memory—assailed her, smothering her with hot embarrassment... and painful yearning.

She shook the weakness off. That evening hadn't been magical, it had been a mistake. He'd had condoms in his bag—more than one—like the carefree casual sex-slayer he was. And they'd used them—reckless yes, but not stupid. But they'd not realised at the time that one had failed.

She blinked and focused on Luke. The best thing to ever hit her life was sitting in the middle of the massive lounge, his worn play mat had been replaced and a vast assortment of new toys were scattered about him—wooden stacking boxes, several soft-looking small balls and some cute carved animals. One of the stewards was kneeling beside him, playing peek-a-boo. At their arrival the steward stood and looked to Javier, who nodded in dismissal, and she swiftly disappeared out of the far door.

'There's a nanny—'

'You've engaged a nanny?' she interrupted

him in a fierce whisper. 'Without even meeting her?'

'I'm meeting *him* now,' Javier explained with exaggerated patience. 'He's one of the men back in the dining room.'

'Him?' Emmy's blood pounded loudly in her ears.

'You have a problem with that?'

'I have a problem with not having any input.' She shook her head. 'And I know what you're going to say—you haven't had any in the last nine months.'

'Calm down, Emmy. Yes, I'm angry and, yes, I'm going to need time, but I'm not completely insensitive. You know Luke best, so I was waiting for you to interview the nanny with me, and there are other CVs we can go through if you're not comfortable with how this one checks out.'

'How did you get him here already?'

'I don't sleep as soundly as you,' he muttered. 'I arranged it through the night.'

The truth was she hadn't slept soundly at all—it had taken hours to fall asleep and when she finally had, she'd been tormented by repeats of that dream.

'But before we interview him, there's someone else who'd like to talk to you briefly,' Javier added before disappearing back down the corridor.

Emmy scooped up Luke and watched worriedly as Javier returned with the older of the two men.

'I've spent a lovely half-hour with your son this morning.' The man smiled at her patronisingly. 'I'm Dr Morales, a children's specialist.'

Emmy forced herself to maintain her smile but she was shocked. Javier had had a *paediatrician* look over their son?

'I only had a couple of questions,' he said amiably enough. 'Has Luke ever been on any regular medication?'

'No, never.' She shook her head. 'He's been very healthy. Only a little grizzly with his first tooth and a small cold once.'

'He's a lovely boy.' The doctor smiled down at her. 'You've cared for him well.'

Emmy was so angry she couldn't think of an adequate response. Fortunately Javier led him away moments later, only to return and tell her it was time to meet the prospective nanny.

That interview process was easy. She sat

Luke on her knee and read over the man's résumé while Javier grilled him to the point that Emmy actually felt bad for the guy. His CV was insanely impressive—not only were there papers on child psychology, nutrition and development in his four-year degree, there were courses in defensive driving, cybersecurity and escaping the paparazzi. It took only moments for her to understand that Javier wouldn't allow anyone on board and near Luke who wasn't utterly overqualified and from some elite school. He was used to the best and expected the best from everyone in his life. And he wanted only the best for his son. It was terrifying.

'Emmy?'

She belatedly realised Javier was waiting for her to ask a question.

'Would you mind a probation period, Thomas?' she asked. 'And if you work under observation with Luke initially?'

'Of course.' He smiled.

Javier looked at her and she nodded. She was shamefully glad that there wasn't going to be a pretty nanny staying with them. She knew it was ridiculous of her. She had no right to be jealous of any imaginary nanny being around

Javier—she had no hold over *him*. It was Luke she was really concerned about. But she wasn't going to lose time with her son. As she had no job the nanny was going to be virtually redundant most of the time. But that wasn't her problem. Javier wanted to make some decisions here, this was one she wouldn't fight.

An hour later Emmy sat with Thomas, the new nanny, as he met Luke. Through the open doorway she saw Javier casually guide Dr Morales to the helicopter that had appeared on the top rear deck. She had no idea how she'd slept through the arrival of a helicopter. Or through the boat engine firing up and moving them so far from her home.

It scared her that Javier had achieved so much so quickly, but she masked her concerns, staying with Luke and the new nanny until it was time for her son to take a nap. Then she stayed until her son fell asleep, quietly talking Thomas through Luke's routines. Eventually a steward appeared and invited Thomas to follow him so he could get a tour of the yacht.

Emmy took the baby monitor she'd discovered with her so she could hear if Luke woke. Then she walked up the stairs to discover

Javier sitting back on the pool deck, looking as if he hadn't a care in the world. As he caught her eye his chin lifted. Something sparked in his expression, as if he'd been waiting for her to find him.

'You know, I don't need your fancy doctor to tell me I've done a good job, like some patronising man…' She inhaled deeply. 'I know I've made mistakes, but I've done the best I could.'

'I know that.' Javier's gaze narrowed on her. 'Maybe the doctor should've checked you over too. You still look tired even though you slept late.'

'It takes more than one night to recover from months of sleep deprivation.' She tried to snatch a breath and calm down, but it was a losing battle. 'I don't need anyone to look me over,' she muttered. 'I'm perfectly healthy.'

'Then it won't be a problem for him to see you. We can recall the chopper—'

'Don't you dare,' she snapped. 'That would be such an invasion of my privacy. I won't have him reporting to you on my well-being.'

'So I'm not to be concerned about you in any way?'

'No. You're not. Stop trying to do the "right" thing all the time.'

'Stop *what*?' He frowned deeply at her. 'You really don't trust my intentions, do you?'

'And you really don't trust me,' she answered. 'I understand it, but to think that Luke might be unwell in some way…? Or that I might have mistreated him…? Or not cared for him properly…? I have put him first in every way I can—' She broke off.

Javier stared at her and slowly shook his head. 'Emerald, I wasn't questioning your capability as a mother.'

'No?' She was so hurt by his action. 'Isn't that exactly what that was?'

'I didn't mean it to be, but I can understand that it might have come across as offensive. I just…' A grim expression tightened his face as he trailed off.

Emmy stared at him impatiently. 'You just what?' She shook her head when he still didn't respond. 'See?' His *so* controlled reticence infuriated her. 'You just don't trust me.'

His expression tightened and he stepped forward. 'I feel compelled to know everything,' he ground out with clear reluctance.

She paused as she heard the raw edge to his admission. 'About Luke?' she clarified softly. 'You can ask me,' she assured him quickly. 'Ask me anything. I want him to have a good relationship with you.'

At that Javier seemed to lose a touch of colour and Emmy stepped closer—was he worried he wasn't going to be a good father to their son?

'I've missed out on so much,' he muttered so softly. 'What if I can't ever make it up...?'

Her heart ached as she realised how much she'd hurt him. She felt appalled at how close she'd come to denying both Javier and Luke this relationship. She should have contacted him. She should have given him the chance. Instinctively she put her hand on his arm in both apology and reassurance.

'He's so young and he's very loving,' she promised.

She felt Javier's muscles tense beneath her touch and suddenly the atmosphere was charged. Before she could lift her hand away he'd clamped his over the top of hers, pressing her palm against his hot skin. He stepped back and sat on the sofa. By the nature of his hold on her, she had to sit too. Right beside him.

Maybe she should have resisted more. But it flickered between them—that shimmering, powerful thing that sent shivers along her nerve-endings and made her hold her breath. That dangerous, beguiling thing.

His gaze was very dark and deep as he smoothed his hand over the back of hers and then flipped hers over to inspect her palm. 'Why did you work so hard?'

'I owed Connie everything,' she answered, trying to mask the sudden tightness in her lungs. 'Without her, I would've had nowhere to go.'

His grip on her tensed and she sought to make him understand somehow.

'We were in a safe, beautiful place, had a roof over our heads, food on the table,' she tried to explain. 'It might not have been perfect—' She broke off at his snort. 'But it was the best I could do.'

'It didn't have to be like that. You didn't have to work all hours…'

She frowned at him. 'But—'

'I would have helped you,' he growled roughly. 'I would have done everything in my power to help you. You didn't *need* to do this on your own.'

Regret rose, smashing down the last of her defences.

'Don't,' she mumbled as that other emotion spilled, overwhelming her to the point where she had to reject him. 'Don't say nice things to me.'

He stared at her for a second. 'Then what should I do?' he asked with the gentlest of tease in his tone. 'Berate you? Bully you? What am I supposed to do?'

'I don't know.'

His sudden soft chuckle was a torturous reminder of the carefree, humorous man she'd met that night. He'd been playful and kind and she'd instinctively trusted him with so very much. And now something wild and free soared again, enabling her to laugh with him in an effervescent release and for just a moment that terrible tension eased. A split second later tears sprang to her eyes.

'I'm sorry,' she whispered. She was truly

sorry she hadn't been able to contact him for so long. And more so that she'd chosen not to when she'd finally found out who he really was.

'I know,' he whispered back, and his beautiful cocoa gaze bored into hers. 'I'm sorry too.'

They'd not meant for this to happen. They'd not meant for a fantasy escape to have such serious repercussions.

'We can move forward,' she breathed.

He stared back at her silently and that charge in the atmosphere strengthened.

But this wasn't what she'd meant. Not this curling heat. She thought they'd just had a breakthrough—but that tiny moment of honesty was now submerged by the need rearing between them again. Intense, unstoppable and inescapable. It was more than a minor itch or low ache. It was a furious hunger and every time she got within five feet of him, it burned. She could barely resist the pull to lean closer still. His hand held hers loosely but she was incarcerated by the spiralling emotions. Flames flickered promise and pleasure. She stared into his eyes and he leaned towards her slowly. Closer, closer still until the conflagration ignited.

'We sh-shouldn't...' She was so breathless now.

But he was so close, his mouth brushed hers even as she tried to speak. 'We sh—'

'Shh,' he commanded and his lips silenced hers.

Her eyes closed and her mouth parted on a sigh of surrender as ecstasy surged through her. She moaned as she felt his answering tremor. His arms went hard and tight around her and she sank against him. In seconds she was utterly breathless, desperate for more. All her cares and concerns—actually all her *brains*—were lost. There was nothing but this touch and the hot fierce temptation that shivered through every cell.

She'd thought she remembered. But she'd not—not the intensity and shimmering raw pleasure to be found right here in his kiss.

She'd never regretted the night she'd spent in his—a stranger's—arms. She'd never questioned her choice to gift him her virginity so swiftly and easily. Because the touch, the pleasure she'd discovered with him, in his body, had been the most ultimate sensation of her life. There'd been no uncertainty, no decision necessary. There'd only been desperation for more. But while swift, it hadn't felt carefree, nothing as easy as that. It had felt *undeniable*.

She'd been overwhelmed then, but the depth of the pleasure now was even sharper. It was as if her body remembered and were starved to the point that it wouldn't allow her to stop this—she literally couldn't pull back until the ultimate release had been gleaned. Her need for his touch was truly shocking—reducing her in this moment to a starving, feral creature, clinging to the source of possible satisfaction.

'Emmy.' With a growl he pulled her closer as if he knew how bad the ache was and he assuaged it only slightly with a powerful press of his body against hers. 'It's okay.'

But it wasn't. She wanted rid of her clothes. She ached for the absolute escape she'd found that night. It was insane that she sought this from the man who posed such a threat to her very soul. Her heart was all and only Luke's, but Javier could take everything else. And it was only that flashing realisation that shocked her from the mists of his seduction.

'*No,*' she cried—ordering herself to obey more than she was telling him.

Javier released her immediately. Except Emmy was so weakened she swayed after him. He swiftly reached out to grip her shoulders hard to steady her and settle her back from him on the sofa.

'I'm sorry,' she whispered. 'That shouldn't have happened.'

She ached when he released his hold on her a second time—her conflicting desires tearing her apart.

'That was inevitable,' he said roughly. 'You know it as well as I. It's still there, Emmy. As strong as it was the day we met. It's a force neither of us seem equipped to deny.' But there was more than a glimpse of triumph in his eyes.

'Well, we have to.' *She* had to.

Once more she'd all but fallen apart from a single touch—his to explore, to take, to pleasure. She couldn't believe the attraction was so intense and that she'd managed to pull back. She had to find a better defence against it. Because doing this again with him could only lead to trouble.

'Prevent biology?' He glanced at her sceptically. 'Nature wants us to procreate. It seems we're good at it.'

'Well, it's not happening again. That was a mistake.'

His lips twitched but he didn't reply.

'Nothing to say?' She wrapped her arms around her waist, hunching on the sofa.

'We have more important things to argue about.' He shrugged.

That was true, but he was good at avoiding *those* conversations, wasn't he?

'There's no mistake here, Emmy,' he said with that cool confidence. 'There's only what feels good. Why wouldn't you want to feel that again?' He watched her for another moment and his smile faded. 'You're tired.' He reached out and stroked her hair. 'So tired. Right?'

His statement stripped the facade from her and suddenly she couldn't move for exhaustion. All the adrenalin from the last twenty-four hours evaporated, leaving her utterly lacking in energy. He stood and stepped away from her. Regret stabbed but that tiredness swamped it out.

'Look, I'm sorry.' He glanced back at her and sighed. 'Just rest here for a bit. Thomas and I will take care of Luke. I won't…' He trailed off and rubbed in the region of his lowest rib. 'Just relax. You can now.'

CHAPTER FOUR

SHE'D BEEN ASLEEP for *hours*.

Javier paced quietly in the shaded part of the deck, holding Luke close to keep him calm. The child had woken a little while ago and, having had a drink, was now happy to be held and quietly talked to. Though admittedly Javier was running out of things to say. He'd walked around pointing out features of the boat, feeling a fool to think a nine-month-old could ever understand. But he had no clue what else to do and he had to start somewhere.

Javier shot Emmy another worried glance. She was too quiet and still. Protectiveness swept over him. Not just towards the small, sleepy child in his arms, but to that woman lying on the plush sofa. He'd never seen her like this. Peaceful, heart-seizingly beautiful, but vulnerable. She left him breathless.

At least she had more colour in her cheeks now. When he'd first walked into that small shop, she'd paled so quickly he'd wondered if she were about to faint. He'd been stunned that she'd been afraid of him. But of course she'd been terrified, given the massive secret she'd kept from him. And frankly, forgiving her for that was a struggle. He'd missed out on much that he couldn't recover.

Anger mixed with regret and that rush of raw, undeniable lust—the one he was constantly fighting. It had struck him sledgehammer-style all those months ago when she'd walked out of the sea like some siren temptation—all hips and breasts and bold, bold curves, fiery hair and gleaming skin. She'd been irresistible and the desire to make her his had been fierce. He'd busted out every ounce of charm he could muster because he'd wanted her so hard. The flare between them had gone so much further, so much faster than he'd anticipated. But his success had also been certain, because he'd seen it in her eyes too—they'd mirrored his own startled fascination. A flicker of electricity had bound them, drawing them closer together.

It had irked that she'd left before saying goodbye and without leaving him any way of contacting her. But he'd been at fault too, arrogantly failing to tell her his true name.

It hadn't crossed his mind that she'd been working on the islands and that he could've found her again easily. At the time he'd been sure she was a tourist and she'd not said anything to contradict the idea. Truthfully they'd not said all that much of meaning. There'd been flirtation and fun and, beneath, the simmering recognition of mutual attraction and unstoppable desire. Though then there'd been a startling confession—of her inexperience. She'd laughed as she'd admitted it—a bubbling sound of surprise, surrender and pure amusement, and the most primal wave of satisfaction had sunk his reason and he'd vowed to please her. There'd been nothing after that but heated magic—every touch better than the promise they'd both felt. And all he wanted now—the one thought consuming him—was to do it again.

But now it was complicated. He rolled his shoulders, irritated by his own changeability. Seeming to sense Javier's tension, Luke rubbed his face with his little hand, his expression crumpling.

'Mamá's just over there,' Javier awkwardly tried to reassure him with a soft whisper. 'See? She's resting.'

She stirred and Javier stilled, watching as she blinked, then she suddenly sat up, her blue eyes wide.

'It's okay,' Javier said huskily. 'He's here. I've got him.'

Her arms lifted automatically and Javier walked over. Emmy cradled the baby against her soft curves. Her cheeks flushed fractionally more and the gentlest of smiles lit her from within.

Javier stared down at them both, unable to step back. After a moment she looked up at him. Her eyes were dreamy blue now she had her child. But as they regarded each other in solemn silence, wariness stole into them and then that altogether different tension twisted again. All he wanted to do was kiss her again.

'You must be hungry.' He forced himself to speak but it emerged as a hoarse mutter.

She nodded, her gaze dropping. He made himself turn and message the staff, cursing his own weakness.

When he turned back, she'd settled Luke

more comfortably on her knee and was looking across the water. 'The engines have stopped. Where are we?'

'Just off the coast of Pinta.'

'This is Pinta?'

He was surprised that she didn't recognise it. 'You've not been here?'

She shook her head.

'But you've been living on the islands for...'

'Just over two years.' She shrugged. 'I've been working.'

'Then perhaps it's time to take a break.' He sat in the deckchair across from the plush sofa she'd slept on, determinedly maintaining distance and respect.

That wariness returned to her eyes. She was right to be cautious, because he was faking being friendly. As if he were some really good guy who wanted to do right by the woman he'd seduced and the baby she'd then had?

If she only knew what was really going through his mind. Here she was, exhausted from caring for their son for months all by herself and all he could think about was how badly he wanted to tumble her back into bed.

He made himself look at his son and it was a good move, because that awkward feeling returned. He had no clue how to become a father. It was partly why he'd wanted a nanny on board so soon, so he had an expert on hand as well as someone to lift a bit of that load from Emerald. Because he sure as hell couldn't do that yet. He wasn't sure he'd ever be able to.

And he needed to know more about her. Now he'd had a chance to think, he wondered what she'd meant about people judging her the second they learned her name? What was it that had made her afraid to seek him out even for financial support for Luke when she clearly desperately needed it? What was she hiding? Because there had to be something and it had to be big.

'What were you going to tell him when he asked?' he tried to ask mildly.

Emmy shifted on the sofa, startled by the raw edge to Javier's question.

'He would have asked eventually,' he added. 'He'd meet other children with involved fathers. He would've wanted to know about his. So what were you planning to tell him?'

Emmy's heart ached as she read that banked emotion in Javier's eyes and heard the husky edge—as if these were questions he hated having to ask. 'I don't know,' she confessed. 'I was avoiding thinking about it.'

She'd told herself that she could be enough on her own. But not to tell Luke about Javier wouldn't have been fair in the long run. And not finding out if Javier was interested in being involved had been wrong. She should have given him the option, but fear had governed her and somehow she had to explain that to him without telling him everything. Because even though he was trying hard now, she had too much to lose to trust him completely.

'I know I should have contacted you as soon as I knew who you were, but I was so tired and I was just...'

'Furious because you thought I'd lied to you deliberately?' He filled in after her long silence. 'Because I had some bad reason for hiding my identity?'

She had known he'd lied and that had hurt. But it wasn't *only* that that had thrown her. It was the discovery of his status and wealth. A surfing tourist she could have handled. But she couldn't compete with what he could offer. She'd been terrified.

'Actually…' she strove for a measure of truth '… I wanted to succeed on my own,' she admitted awkwardly. 'I didn't want anything—not just from you, but from *anyone*. I was so sick of…' She shook her head, hating having to confess this and unable to articulate it properly. 'I decided I could manage. Luke would be mine and I would be his and we wouldn't need anyone else. I never wanted us to need anyone else. I thought—hoped—that I could be enough for him and that I could do a good job.' To her total mortification, tears spiked on her eyelashes and she furiously blinked them away. 'I didn't want you accusing me of trapping you. Everyone always thinks the worst. The things a couple of people said when they found out I was pregnant… One actually insinuated he was Lucero's baby because I'd named him after him. So I wanted to prove that I could do this on my own. I think I lost perspective.' She drew in a shaking breath. 'But that wasn't fair on Luke and it wasn't fair on you and I'm sorry.'

He was silent for a long moment.

'I accept your apology,' he said formally. 'And I'm sorry I lied that night. I have no real excuse other than I just wanted a night off from being me. I'm sorry I didn't try harder to track you down when I came back. I'm sorry you've been doing this alone all this time.' He stepped closer. 'And I'm sorry I made you feel like you were being judged, or that I was patronising you when I brought in that doctor. But I'm not patronising you now. I'm just being honest. Luke is an amazing little boy and that's all because of you.'

She stared up at him, feeling the fragility of this peace offering and longing to accept it. To believe in it. To hope that perhaps they could make this work. But then she remembered that he knew nothing of who she really was. And when he discovered that shame of her past? She forced her gaze towards the azure water. She couldn't trust that the truth wouldn't be used to take Luke from her.

'Señor Torres?'

Relief and regret hit in equal measure as a steward interrupted them to deliver a platter of fresh fruit, cheese and cold cuts. Emmy snaffled a piece of apple, savouring its juicy freshness and the distraction it provided, and gave Luke one of the baby crackers that had been thoughtfully put on the plate.

'So why were you angry when you learned who I was?' Javier asked after a bit. 'Was it because I'd bought Lucero's property? Or because I'd lied?'

Her nerves tightened. He was so far out of her league—wealthy and powerful—she'd been sure he'd take Luke from her if he knew. He still could.

She needed more time to figure out how she could convince him that she was a good influence on Luke's life. So she diverted her answer. 'I loved Lucero's property how it was—the age of the old hostel, that old boathouse and the value of his foundation for getting volunteers to help keep everything around here pristine. I know it was a little run-down, but I was afraid of what you're going to do with it.'

'But isn't it a good thing for that property to be developed? You must know Lucero wanted it cared for,' he said. 'He didn't have the energy or resources to do it himself. He trusted that to me.'

'To you?' Her stomach dropped. 'You met him?'

'I returned a few months after...' He cleared his throat. 'I was looking for an opportunity here and approached him when I learned he owned that property.'

Javier had been back to the Galapagos before now? And she'd not run into him?

'But I would've known if you'd seen Lucero,' she said, trying to reject the terrible regret rising within her. 'I was his carer round the clock towards the end.'

Javier frowned. 'He told me his carer was called Esme. She was visiting another island when I was there.'

She gasped. 'He called me Esmerelda when he was being grand—Esme for short.'

'Esme. Emerald...' He muttered something indecipherable beneath his breath and then looked at her with a rueful shake of his head.

That shimmering electricity fluttered between them. Fate. It had failed them that time.

'So why did you name our son after him?' he asked quietly.

That question was easy. 'Because he was a good man,' she said simply. 'He gave me a home and I hadn't had one in a while.' She fell silent, realising what she'd just admitted and hoping Javier wouldn't ask why. She rubbed little Luke's back as he sucked on the cracker and quickly thought of a question of her own. 'Why did you want the hostel?' she asked. 'Was it just the location?'

'Mmm.' Now Javier glanced away, his gaze skimming the blue waters. 'Why not go for a swim?' he suggested. 'It's a beautiful afternoon. It'll refresh you after the sleep.'

She shook her head and looked down at Luke in her lap, disappointed by him avoiding directly answering her.

'I'll hold him while you're out there,' Javier offered, and then rolled his eyes at her continued hesitation. 'I promise not to make off with him when you're half a mile from the boat.'

She half chuckled. 'You're not going to turn on the engines and leave me in the middle of the ocean?'

'Of course not,' he said. 'Maybe *you* might try to trust *me*?'

She couldn't hold his gaze for long; the gleam

in his eyes threatened to mesmerise her all over again. And the regret she felt?

'I'm not going to hurt him, Emmy.'

'I know,' she muttered with a sad shake of her head. 'I never thought you would.'

She was the one who was going to be hurt. She'd feared it from the moment she'd found out his true identity, and from the second he'd walked back into her life she'd known it would be inevitable.

'Then give him to me and go get changed.'

The water was tempting and she desperately needed to cool down and regain some thinking time. She hadn't taken a proper swim in so long; she'd always had Luke with her. But there was a kind of freedom she only felt in the water. And she knew Javier understood that—they'd bonded over it that night they'd been together.

Down in her cabin, she realised her old green bikini didn't fit as well as it once had. She covered up by draping one of the large, soft towels in her private bathroom around her and then walked out to the rear deck.

Javier was there holding Luke and they were sporting matching floppy-brimmed hats, casting their faces in the shade. Javier's gaze glittered as she dropped the towel and put it on the top step.

'I can't tell you how many times I've thought about that bikini,' he said huskily.

Emmy swallowed hard and she pretended she hadn't heard him. The thinnest tendril of trust was blossoming between them, but that raging physical need threatened to overshadow—or stomp on—that tender shooting stem. She pressed her lips together, holding in the sharp yearning to turn and lean against his body. As crazy, as wrong as it was, she couldn't deny her desire. But she could try to ignore it.

She turned her back, hiding how her heavy breasts had tightened in response to his mere look. They were almost too big for the stretchy fabric encasing them. She stepped down, bracing in the cold water. She struck out strongly, swimming hard, then dived beneath the clear waves. She'd missed this so much—the total liberation as she submerged and let the cold soothe her heated skin.

Animals, as always in this remote, fascinating part of the world, came close. Curious and unafraid and enchanting—tortoise, sea lions, birds. A weight slipped free, letting her float and enjoy the serene peace of the sea.

Eventually she returned to the boat, climbing up the stairs that made it so easy to get in and out. Physically tired but happy, she wrapped herself in the towel.

Javier had retreated up to the pool deck and was now sprawled with Luke on the shaded sofa. As Emmy walked up to check on Luke, she warily glanced at Javier—had she taken too long? His expression was unreadable behind the sunglasses he'd put on. 'I haven't swum like that in ages, thank you for that,' she said.

Javier didn't answer but Luke gurgled.

'Let me have him.' Impulsively she let her towel fall. 'He loves the water.'

Javier leaned forward. 'He swims already?'

Emmy undressed Luke and lifted him into the warmer water of the onboard pool with her. Luke squawked happily as she swished him through the water. Javier stood at the pool's edge and watched, a smile slowly spreading over his face. Emmy's heart bumped as she heard him laugh. The carefree humour reminded her of that first night. 'You want to hold him?'

She didn't wait for him to answer, she just handed Luke to him.

Javier laughed throatily as Luke bounced excitedly in his arms and wet him completely.

'You mind if I come in with you?' he asked huskily.

'Of course not.' Her mouth dried as she took Luke back from him.

Javier's shirt had got wet from wrestling with their wriggling, giggling, soaked son. She tried not to gape as he peeled it from his body, but it was then impossible not to stare at his rippling muscles as he entered the water and took Luke from her again. The fiercest wave of heat engulfed her at the sight of him engaging with their son. A primal, powerful surge of feminine pride followed—he was the father of her child, he was her *mate*—and her body wanted him again.

Except he *wasn't* hers.

She stepped out of the pool and into the shade, embarrassed by the fierce reaction of her body at the sight of Javier in nothing but swim shorts. That earlier, incendiary kiss lingered on her lips like an illicit sizzle and she wanted another burn.

He laughed lightly again. 'He's a natural,' he called to her. 'No surprise given he's your son.'

Emmy couldn't answer because her heart was in her throat.

Fortunately Javier then called for the nanny. Thomas appeared and capably swept Luke into a massive, soft towel.

'I think he's ready for a tidy-up and a snack,' Javier said smoothly to Thomas and then glanced at Emmy. 'We need time to relax over dinner.'

'Of course.'

Emmy anxiously watched Thomas take Luke inside. But it wasn't that she didn't trust the man with her baby, it was that she didn't trust herself to be alone with her son's father.

CHAPTER FIVE

EMMY WAITED FOR the last page to emerge from the printer and then gathered the leaves of paper together. She'd been in the blindingly well-equipped onboard office for two hours but she was finally done. She stood and stretched in a fruitless attempt to ease the tension from her body.

She'd tried talking to Javier about light things at dinner last night—but the monosyllabic replies she'd got from the most innocuous of questions had swiftly taught her that he wasn't interested in opening up. And perhaps that was good. So she'd then been careful, keeping conversation utterly focused on Luke, and she'd escaped to her suite as soon as they'd put him to bed. She couldn't trust herself around Javier. Not after that kiss. Apparently he was her personal Kryptonite and when she was around him, all rational capacity to think fled, leaving her as little more than a ball of raw desire. To be so undone by hormones was mortifying. The only way to get through it with even a smidge of dignity was to keep her distance.

She knew she needed to let Javier have time with Luke without her hovering as if afraid he were about to make off with him. He needed to forge his own relationship with his son. She'd denied them both that for too long and felt terrible about it.

In the middle of the night—when her stupid brain wouldn't shut down—she'd thought of one small way she might alleviate some of his loss, but now she'd finished, she was nervous about giving it to him.

She walked through to the pool deck to find Javier alone with Luke. She stopped in the doorway, somewhat stunned to see him engaged in the task of finishing up a nappy change.

He glanced up. 'What?' he sounded defensive.

'You did a good job.' The second she said it she realised she sounded as patronising to him as that doctor had been to her yesterday. But she hadn't meant to be. Javier had said he hadn't meant to either. She was prickly and too defensive and right now so was he.

'The first time I put his nappy on backwards,' she admitted with a shy smile. 'The nurse in the hospital broke it to me so kindly and then showed me how to do it properly.'

Javier sat back and a rueful expression softened the hardness in his eyes. 'I looked up instructions online.'

'Really?' Her grin widened.

'And I checked with Thomas for good measure.' He lifted his son back down to his play mat, where he immediately crawled over to his favourite toy, sat down and stuck it in his mouth.

'You did?' Emmy was surprised. 'You seem so capable, like you're just naturally brilliant at everything you attempt, first time.'

'No.' He laughed softly. 'Definitely not.'

She didn't believe him. He had that aura of surety about him.

'Most people need to try things a couple of times before they get the hang of it,' he said lightly, but his gaze was unwavering and unbearably intense.

Suddenly the most inappropriate recollection

ran in her head. To make it worse, she had the suffocating feeling he sensed exactly what it was that she was remembering.

Their night. Her first times—*all* of them with him. And that intimacy, that sweetness, had turned so hot. She'd adored the muffled laughter that they'd shared before she could only moan. It had been the ultimate seduction.

'I have something for you,' she said, desperately changing the subject so she wouldn't be blinded into brainlessness by that smile. Her face burned as she held out the slim booklet she'd hidden behind her back. He took it from her, his eyebrows lifting in silent query.

'My phone isn't that great, but I took snaps of Luke all the time this year. Like, hundreds of photos,' she babbled nervously. 'I thought you might like some…'

She trailed off as Javier opened the booklet to the first page and then flicked to the next. And suddenly she worried that it would upset him somehow.

'I didn't do it to make you see what you've missed…' She bit her lip anxiously, watching him go through the booklet.

He was too quiet. Did he hate it?

'I hope it's okay I asked the staff if you had a printer on board,' she explained.

It turned out there was an entire office suite that was stocked with all the stationery imaginable, including photo paper. She'd borrowed a computer and loaded the photos, compiling and printing them into a small book using a graphics platform—adding captions beneath to explain how old Luke had been and what the milestone or moment was. It hadn't taken long. The hardest part had been picking which of the many pictures she'd use. She'd even bound it with a piece of ribbon she'd found. But staring at it now, as Javier went through it page by page, ever so slowly, it looked flimsy and excruciatingly home-made.

Embarrassment burned from her skin, through every vital organ and deep into her bones.

'We can get them printed professionally, of course,' she muttered hopelessly. 'I just wanted you to have the pictures now. There are loads more. I've put them all onto that computer for you, so you have them digitally as well.'

She felt appallingly vulnerable watching him silently turn each page, inspecting each picture she'd selected. Luke having his first bath. His playful smile. On his tummy. Playing in the sand. Javier went all the way through the booklet to the final page and then returned to the first one. It was a black and white shot and it was the only one that featured her as well.

'I just included that because it's the very first picture of him,' she explained in a rushing whisper. 'One of the nurses in the hospital took it moments after he was born.'

A very tiny Luke was lying on her chest. She'd been vain enough to print it in black and white so the ravages of childbirth were less obvious on her face. Not that Javier would want pictures of *her*, of course, but his son. And this pretty much was his son's first moment alive in the world.

'Thank you for this,' he said quietly. 'The photos are beautiful.'

Awkwardly she bent and put together a few of the loose toys, just to avoid looking at him. 'I have an app on my phone to override the usual camera settings and amp up the results a bit.'

'You took these on your phone?' he asked.

She nodded.

'You have a good eye for composition.'

'It helps that I'm completely in love with my subject,' she muttered dryly. Her son was the absolute light and joy of her life. 'I have hundreds—you can have them all. I take them, not to get some stylised perfect shot, but to bring that moment back. The emotions, the story behind that stupid pose, or why I was out looking at the sunset that day…an aide-memoire, you know? Not for anyone else but me.' She realised she was babbling. 'Sorry to be boring.'

'I'm not bored. I want to see the photos. I want you to tell me the stories behind them.'

She glanced down at him and then narrowed her gaze. Her little boy was sitting with a curiously fierce expression on his face. She smothered her spreading smile.

'What is it?' Javier noticed her reaction and turned to survey Luke's stillness on the mat.

'Uh,' she half laughed beneath her breath. 'I think he's testing your nappy skills.'

'Seriously?' Javier looked miffed. 'I just changed it.'

Emmy leaned forward and sniffed delicately.

'Um...well, he needs another change.' She stood.

'I'll do it.' Javier scooped Luke up. 'But I think we need to be in the nursery.'

Emmy hesitated. 'You don't want Thomas to handle this one?' She followed him through to the nursery. 'The poor guy's twiddling his thumbs down on the crew deck.'

'Dream job.' Javier sent her an ironically amused glance. 'I figure, if I can handle this...'

He was determined to learn and be hands-on, not just seeing Luke as 'his' in the sense of a possession. And while that ought to please her and she knew it was best for her baby, it scared her too. What if eventually Luke chose Javier over her? She wouldn't blame him, not when his father could give him so much more than she ever could. She braced against the insecurity eating away at her insides. She had to be better than this—for Luke if nothing else.

'Do you want me to take a photo of you two, when he's decent again?' She bit her lip as she waited for Javier's answer. 'You know, as an aide-memoire for this moment?'

Javier's hands stilled and he glanced her. 'Sí, thanks.' He bent over Luke and smothered a groan. 'But I hope we have gas masks some-where.'

She chuckled and went to fetch her phone. With his permission she'd take photos any chance she could…mentally working on part two of his photo book. But when she returned, Javier had finished and he passed Luke to her.

'He needs you. He's starting to fret.'

Luke curled against her, his grizzling in-stantly silenced. 'He's just tired,' she explained a little guiltily to Javier.

'It's okay, Emmy. I know it's going to take a little time.'

She shifted Luke to her hip and turned away from that look in his eyes. She was a fool for reading double meanings into everything he said. Javier wanted to build a relationship with *Luke*, not with her, yet she couldn't help hop-ing—and then couldn't help glancing back up to see if there was something to read in his eyes.

But he then stepped back and turned away, shutting her out again. 'I'll go and see if lunch is ready.'

Emmy sank onto the cushions by the pool and cuddled her sleepy son, feeling as if she

needed to take another dip to cool off and battle the insane disappointment that Javier had
gone inside. But that aching wouldn't seem to
stop; it was a tension she couldn't ease no matter how hard she tried.

Javier tried not to stare at Emmy as they sat in
the shade and lunched on ceviche while Luke
slept. He wasn't really tasting the fish, he was
too consumed by curiosity—unable to stop
himself from studying her intently.

She was avoiding looking at him by watching the sea. The longing in her eyes had barely
been masked yesterday and it had been the
same today. Her love for the water had been
the first thing he'd noticed about her. Okay,
the second thing. But the sensual pleasure
she took in it, he felt too. She was that siren,
the mermaid he'd been unable to resist…the
fierce dragon woman who'd breathed fire when
aroused.

On one level he agreed with her that they
shouldn't touch again. That kiss yesterday had
burned his brain to ash. There was too much
for them to navigate without getting distracted
by lust. He'd thought he could put it aside until

he'd got to spend some time with his son and figured out how they were going to make their future work. But it turned out that he couldn't concentrate on any of that far more important stuff. The spark they shared was too strong. So now he wondered if he needed to take the opposite strategy. Maybe if they cleared the air of this sexual tension, then they could focus on what was really important?

Not going to lie, it was a far more appealing prospect.

It had been like this that first night too. As inevitable as the setting of the sun. Sheer biology—animal attraction and all that. He didn't think either of them were going to be able to deny their chemistry for too much longer. So why fight it? Why not give in and get it gone? Why not feel good together this one way in which they could?

It was obvious she was struggling with it too, given she was either avoiding him altogether or gazing at him with that slightly dazed expression. It amused and provoked and made him ache to haul her close and be done with it.

But his intellectual curiosity about her was growing hourly—he had a million questions and she was avoiding answering any of them in any real depth. The only thing he could tell for certain was her love for Luke. He'd seen the anxiety in her eyes when first watching him interact with the baby. And her hovering over Thomas in those first few hours. Not to mention the screeds of information she'd then given both of them about Luke's likes and dislikes and demeanour. She'd taken such good care of him that Javier suspected there was nothing she wouldn't do for their baby. And that was balm on the irritated welts inside him.

The photo book she'd made had rendered him speechless, touching a sensitivity within that he'd not been aware he even had. His first instinct regarding Luke had been to ensure his physical safety, to determine his nearness so that he could give the child all he could offer. Because he knew that what he could offer was mostly material things. But now that the baby was on board, Javier was at a loss where to start in terms of building an actual relationship. He had no idea how to parent a small person. All he knew was that he'd like to do a better job than his parents had—he could only hope he was capable of it.

His father had opted for the straight abandonment approach, walking out when he was only five. While his mother had gone for the outsourcing angle—packing him off to boarding school so she could focus on forming her new family with her new man.

Surely just by being around Javier could screw his own child up a little less than he'd been? Just by actually being interested?

So he'd studied each photo several times—soaking up details. But always he returned to that first shot of Emerald and Luke together. The image set something twisting alight in his gut. So many conflicting emotions—not just jealousy and anger but pride and awe and absolute regret.

He should've been there. He should've had the chance to share in that amazing moment. He'd not known how much he could want something the way he wanted that. But the underlying lick of doubt about his suitability for parenthood curled and grew larger—was it too late already? Being *absent*, he felt, was the worst way he could have begun.

And despite all that internal chaos, he still couldn't get past his physical desire for her.

His mind circled beyond the reach of his control, returning to his want for her. His body never failed to tighten in response to her presence. He wasn't *vulnerable* to anyone—he'd learned to keep his emotions in check ever since he was a small child packed off to boarding school, scolded for showing emotion, constantly being lectured about how lucky he was, how grateful he should be. But he knew the reality beneath that 'luckiness' of his. His father had left him and then he'd been sent away because he'd not been wanted by his mother either. Because he'd not been wanted, he'd not fitted into the new mould. He'd learned to keep his ambitions his own and his definition of success and fulfilment utterly within his own power and control. No one else would have the power to impact on what *he* wanted and achieved in his life. It was very simple and up till now it had worked.

But his desire for Emmy had kept him awake for so many nights. It had stopped him sleeping with anyone else for over a year. He'd decided he was bored and tired of meaningless one-night stands—that they weren't satisfactory. But that one-night stand with Emmy had been insanely satisfactory. And that was the problem. His recollection of it was amplified, right? It had become too big and was now blown out of all proportion. He needed to slay the dragon it had become.

He needed to get rid of it. They both did. There was really only one way for them to do that. And then it would be gone. Anticipation shot adrenalin into his muscles. They tensed and primed. His whole damn body ached.

'I think I'll have another quick swim.' She avoided his gaze as she stood, as if she somehow sensed his intentions. 'Take advantage while Luke is sleeping.'

'Running away again?' he called softly.

'Pardon?' She turned back to him warily.

'You're running away.'

She faced him squarely. 'We're on a boat in the middle of the ocean. There's nowhere to run to.'

'Yet you're doing it remarkably well.'

'Meaning?'

'Meaning you're very careful not to be alone with me. You're constantly using Luke as your chaperone.'

She stilled, seeming to draw a slow breath

before lifting her chin to face him squarely. 'Luke is the only reason we're in the same space again. There's no need for us to spend time together when he's not awake.'

He laughed. 'You actually think that?'

'I actually think that's what's best.' She nodded. 'For all of us.'

'You're that afraid?' he asked softly.

Emmy couldn't deny it—it was the truth after all. She'd managed to avoid being alone with Javier much in these last few hours, sensing her self-control slipping. He devastated her—reducing her to nothing but a wanting, willing piece of woman. It was mortifying.

'You don't think it would be best for Luke if you and I got to know each other better?' he added.

That was the *last* thing she wanted and she suspected it was the last thing he really meant. 'I don't think it's necessary.'

'You said only yesterday that we needed to talk.'

'I've changed my mind. And I don't think *talking* is what you're meaning now, either,' she challenged bravely.

A teasing half-smile lit his eyes and he offered a shrug. 'We're going to be co-parenting that little boy together for the rest of our lives. I think it's imperative we get past platitudes, Emerald.'

'Well, what is it you wish to know?' she asked flippantly—as if she had nothing to hide, nothing to care so deeply about that she couldn't express it. She could pretend she came from a normal family.

'Okay.' He tilted his head and studied her intently. 'Where are your parents?' He watched her steadily. 'Why are you taking care of your child all on your own miles and miles away from your homeland?'

Her heart thudded at the pinpoint accuracy of his questioning.

'Don't you want your own mother to help you out?' he asked.

She couldn't tell him the complete truth, but perhaps she could escape with partial facts. 'We're not close.'

'I got that impression,' he said wryly. 'Why is that?'

She shrugged. 'It's just the way it is. My parents are closer to my brother. I always had itchy feet—a yearning to travel—and when I came here, I fell in love with the islands. You must agree there's something magical about them.'

'Yes, there is.' He watched her, waiting for more. When she said nothing, he frowned. 'When did you first start travelling?'

'As a teenager,' she answered cagily.

'Oh?'

She nodded. 'Always curious, that was me.' But she saw the scepticism in his eyes.

'How did you get the money to travel?'

Her pride was flicked and her defensiveness sparked a more detailed, honest answer. 'I've always had part-time jobs, always paid my own way or worked for bed and board. I've worked on voluntary projects for years. I've got quite good at them.'

'You didn't want to study past school?'

She'd not had the luxury of that choice, but she'd recovered enough equilibrium to know she couldn't tell him that. 'I didn't finish school, let alone get a college degree.'

She sat back, waited for the judgement to begin.

But he too eased back in his seat, a speculative gleam in his eye. 'I dropped out of university.'

'Really?' She was startled.

'Uh-huh.' He nodded. 'I could tell you I didn't have time to waste studying because there was too much money to be made with my entrepreneurial brilliance.' He eased the arrogance with a wink. 'But that's only the braggy bit, not the actual truth.'

She couldn't help smiling. 'Go on, then, what's the actual truth?'

'I was betrayed,' he said simply with a shrug, looking down to veil his eyes. 'Which, I guess, is partly why I was so touchy about you keeping Luke from me. I'd been lied to before about important things and I dislike the feeling immensely.'

Her curiosity bloomed. 'Who—?'

'So, I guess our nanny has more qualifications than the both of us put together.' He overrode her next, most inevitable question with a teasing smile. 'Maybe we made a good choice with him?'

'Maybe, yes.' Emmy gazed at the water again as a sense of intimacy that had swirled for just a second was vaporised by his determined diversion.

That morsel of personal information had

only intrigued her more and she'd wanted to ask about his own parents too, but he'd swiftly stopped that conversation from continuing. And perhaps that was a good thing? She was intensely drawn to him, but she still couldn't trust him enough to let her guard down fully. If he knew everything about her—if he knew the criminal history of her parents and her brother, and her own lie? He'd use it all against her in the end. And there *would* be an end to this—in only eighteen months, which suddenly seemed awfully soon. She *had* to step back.

'Am I allowed to go take that swim now?' she asked roughly.

'You need my permission?'

She lifted her chin, determined to put their dealings back to the bargain they'd struck. 'These eighteen months are yours, isn't that correct?'

His cocoa and coffee eyes lit with a challenge she refused to identify—yet she couldn't turn away from it.

'If that's how you want to view it,' he replied roughly. 'For the next eighteen months, your presence is mine.'

CHAPTER SIX

EMMY DIVED BENEATH the water and emerged
to take a deep breath but the cool didn't calm
her the way she needed it to. That fact was just
crazy—she was swimming in a gorgeous lap
pool on a luxurious superyacht in the middle
of the world's most beautiful destination and
she *ought* to be able to relax. Instead she was
more tense than ever, and she was angry—with
herself and with him—for her curiosity and his
reticence and that infernal, eternal wretched
desire that couldn't seem to be suffocated suc-
cessfully by either of them.

She swam a few short lengths, anything to
burn off some of her nervous energy. But when
she stood to take breath again, she discovered
Javier at the end of the pool—wearing nothing but black swimming shorts.

'What are you doing?' She glared at him in
surprise. She'd only been away from him for

five minutes and it *really* wasn't long enough for her to cool down to safe mode.

'What does it look like?' he challenged. 'Or are you the only one allowed to enjoy swimming in the water?' Something familiar glinted in his eyes. 'This isn't a private beach today, Emmy. This is my boat and it's my pool.'

'And it's your requirement that I'm here,' she tossed at him. 'So you'll have to put up with me taking up half the space.'

But she knew the pool wasn't big enough for them both. No pool would be big enough. He'd still be too near, with his bared, honed body—all muscle, strength and speed. He was built for physical dominance and endurance and her mouth really ought not to have dried at the sight of him. But it had. She felt tight and too aware, but she stretched her arms out wide along the edge of the pool and let her feet float up in front to pretend she was fabulously relaxed. She refused to curl into something smaller or escape the water entirely as she suddenly felt compelled to do. She couldn't let him chase her away entirely. More precisely, she refused to let her own stupid, treacherous body chase her away. She could control her own urges, couldn't she?

She was going to need to—she had Luke to consider.

Javier lazily walked down the steps into the water, his gaze unerringly on hers, a small smile curving his lips. Emmy's core temperature soared higher with each step he took.

She released a pent-up breath when he finally submerged fully into the water and swam— it took a single stroke to propel him from one end of the pool to another, he was that powerful. But even so, she felt as if there were something leashed about his movements. He emerged with a flick of his head and water sprayed towards her.

Yes, this situation was intolerable. She waded towards the stairs.

'You're a liar.'

His low mutter halted her. She sank back into the water, turning to lean against the wall again. 'What have I lied about?'

Of course he'd think something distrusting. He—like almost everyone in her life—would think her guilty of anything and everything. Eventually.

He took hold of her shoulders and stared into her eyes for a long time, and then his gaze lowered to her lips. 'When you said this won't happen again.'

He too was tense and the water cast a sheen over his burnished skin, magnifying the magnificence of all the muscles on show. He was a heady feast for every one of her senses. And every one of them clamoured for her to get closer. But the only thing she could actually do was freeze. She had the horrible feeling that if she went to move, it would only be to get closer to him. Not to escape his presence at all.

At that moment the truth slid free. She couldn't resist her desire for him any longer. She didn't ache for his touch, she burned for it. Restless and hot, she was unable to control her thoughts, unable to calm that reckless yearning inside. She couldn't think straight any more.

'Emmy.'

His harsh growl melted her bones. She couldn't swim away from him. Couldn't stop staring at him. Still leaning back against the pool wall, she was barely able to keep herself afloat.

'Will you just come closer?' he muttered heavily. 'Have mercy on me.'

She shook her head, her throat too tight to allow speech. She couldn't seem to catch her breath, couldn't control the pace of her heart, couldn't resist.

And he knew it.

'Have mercy on you?' she echoed, thunderstruck.

'Emmy.' His warning was low and slow and his desire imperative.

Her lips parted but still sound failed to emerge. Instead she wanted something else. Her gaze locked on his mouth—it too was parted as he drew in a deep, steadying breath.

'I'm going to kiss you, Emmy.'

He had to have felt the tremble that shivered through her body at his words.

'Is that okay?' he asked.

She couldn't answer, she could barely nod her assent. But it was enough and his mouth was on hers at last.

'It's been so long,' he groaned.

Because he knew, as well as she, that she wasn't saying 'no' this time. This time, there was no stopping until they were both beyond satisfied. And so she sank into the kiss. Arms entwined, breathless, she pressed against him. He hoisted her up and sat her on the edge of the pool, parting her legs so he could stand close between them, his face now before her breasts.

She looked down in a heated stupor as he glanced back up at her before returning his attention to feast on her body. Her nipples strained tight and hard against her bikini. His shallow breathing teased her as he leaned closer to her neck. Her eyes closed and she fell almost into a delirium as his hot mouth stroked over her skin.

He pressed wide, hot kisses down her neck, across her collarbones briefly before plundering lower, across her décolletage to where her curves were swollen and waiting. Through the wet fabric he sucked her into the hot cavern of his mouth. She cried out, but it wasn't enough for him, or her. He growled as he deftly pulled her bikini top away and her unfettered breasts swayed with newfound freedom. She gasped as he cupped them with wide hands, growling again with feral pleasure as her curves overflowed his hold. He pressed his hands closer, squeezing so her nipples were pushed up even more prominently, lifting them towards his hungry gaze.

'Javier,' she panted as he bent and rasped his tongue across each taut nub. Her hips shifted, her need for this kind of attention further south. For him to ease both their hungers, not by mere tasting, but devouring. But he was focused on the slow, physical worship of her breasts first. He sucked gently at first, then harder—ravenously—until she moaned, almost blindly clutching his head to her body. Desperately needing the damp, low ache to be assuaged. This was too slow. She'd been tipped into the depths of an almost insane desire too soon.

'I'm here,' he muttered, working his hand between them, feeling her slickness as he brushed his fingers intimately against her.

'Oh, no,' she moaned desperately, arching against his hand to give him greater access. Because that instant was all it took for a powerful orgasm to rush her.

'Oh, yes,' he growled with savage triumph.

His rough laugh provided the baseline to her high cry of release. His gaze glittered into hers, magnifying the intensity as tremors of ecstasy racked her body. Dazed, she stared back up at him, locked in the seductive spell he'd cast her into too easily, her mouth parted in sensual supplication as she rode the last of the shudders his fingers had so easily summoned from deep within.

'Please,' she whispered brokenly with a shiver of tender pining.

He answered with a passionate kiss, instinctively understanding what she needed now. His tongue slid against hers with the commanding possession she ached for everywhere. She kissed him back furiously, even as the ebbing orgasm leeched the last of her energy, because she didn't want this to end yet. Her lax legs spread wider and she moaned in the back of her throat as he plundered her mouth. She was hot and slick and soft and so utterly his. But even this achingly gorgeous fulfilment wasn't enough.

She'd wanted it beyond belief, yet was devastated that it was over so soon. She'd come so quickly and they weren't even naked. Now she was limp and forlorn because she'd hit that high too fast and she still wanted more despite her sudden exhaustion. She didn't want it to be over.

'Emmy,' he murmured, his lips gently brushing hers. 'Open your eyes,' he ordered softly with another kiss.

The fluttering feelings deep in her belly resurged. She needed all of him. Tension bracketed his mouth, but he smiled as she finally looked at him.

'You want to see my cabin?' he invited with a teasing look in his eyes.

She welcomed the slide into humour and responded instinctively. 'You want to show me the soft furnishings?'

His smile faded. 'You know, I've thought about it a lot since I found you and Luke. I realise now the condoms in my wallet that day were really, really old.' He shook his head, his gaze sombre. 'That was my responsibility. My fault. I'm sorry.'

'I'm not sorry,' she muttered fiercely. 'I'll never be sorry for having Luke.'

'I know. I'm not either.' He nodded and his lips twisted. 'I've got new ones in my room, okay?'

It was a risk but one she couldn't resist. She ached for that complete intensity. 'Okay.'

He took her hand and walked with her up the short flight of stairs to the master deck. At the top, Emmy paused to stare and take it all in.

'You have your own pool up here?' She glanced at him with a reproachful tease in her eyes.

'It's only a dip pool. I can't actually *swim* in it much.' He sent her a smile. 'Though there's a spa as well, if you're interested.'

It was insanely luxurious. She licked her dried lips. 'Maybe later.'

The master suite was incredible. Floor-to-ceiling windows offered a view of the ocean, but with the push of a button silk curtains covered them, leaving her feeling as if the rest of the world had vanished and there was only the two of them in this sumptuous, private space. She glanced at the bed—wider than any she'd ever seen and covered with gorgeous soft-looking linen. The photo book she'd made for him was open on the bedside table, displaying that first picture—the one taken moments after Luke's birth where he was swaddled and lying on her chest in the hospital bed. She looked exhausted but was smiling. It had been the most humbling moment of her life.

'You look beautiful in that photo,' he said gruffly.

She turned to face him.

He tugged down his swimming shorts, kicking them aside to stand before her naked, aroused and proud. He gazed at her, his expression hot and hard as his body was. 'Do you want me, Emmy?'

'You know I do,' she muttered.

She didn't need to say it. He could see it, smell it, taste it, feel it. Just as she could in him—in his eyes, his aroused body.

She walked towards him, letting her hands slide from her ribs down her side to her waist and then to her hips. With a confidence she'd never felt around anyone else, she hooked her thumbs into the band of her bikini bottoms and slowly slipped the fabric south.

He stood, transfixed, the passion in his eyes flaring as he watched her bare herself to him completely. 'You have the most lush body.' He groaned as she stopped in front of him. 'So gorgeous.' He reached out to cup her with feral wonderment. 'Just enough woman for me.'

'Just enough?' She shivered with a laugh. She was so far from skinny her breasts were spilling over his hands.

But he nodded with rapacious fervour and stroked his thumbs across her aching peaks. 'Soft and strong and all mine.'

She liked that he appreciated her curves—there were enough of them, after all—and his untamed, possessive hunger stirred her own appetite for all of him.

It shimmered between them. Memories surged, melding with the present as they moved simultaneously towards each other and rediscovered exactly how well they worked together.

She twisted, entwined with him on the glorious bed. It was the first time they'd had such soft luxury. That night on the beach, it had been on the floor of an abandoned boathouse.

'I've never been this aroused,' he muttered hoarsely. 'I'm trying to slow it down, but I don't know if—' He broke off with a sharply inhaled breath, his eyes closing as tension locked his jaw.

She'd thought she remembered this. But the reality was another shift altogether. She slid her hands to his hips, tugging him closer. Arching. Yearning. She couldn't get enough of the passion he poured into kissing her. Breathless she stirred beneath him, aching for him to move closer. She heard his laugh again, hot and hard and ending in a growl as he kissed down her body. She writhed in utter abandonment until he clamped his hands on her hips and held her still for him to savour.

'It's been so damn long,' he muttered with angry passion before he pressed his mouth to her in the most intimate kiss ever. Torturing her with carnal delight until her breathing broke, until she threaded her hands through his hair and clung tightly on as best she could, until her heat rose, steaming her vision.

'Could you please...?' She couldn't finish her sentence. She could only arch her hips towards him again and again.

'Please what?' He paused and teased.

'Not stop!' she cried. 'Please. Not. Stop!'

He laughed at her loss of language. And then he wasn't just kissing her, he was devouring her. Until all she could do was lie there like the willing supplicant she was—hot and wet and his to eat until desperation for everything he had overwhelmed her.

'Please,' she begged, thrashing her head from side to side. 'Please...please...please...'

'Are you ready for me, Emmy?'

'Yes.' She gasped as he rose and pressed powerfully between her soft thighs.

He was big and strong. She'd thought she remembered, but that searing memory was nothing on the deliciously full sensation as he finally thrust, taking his place within her again. With that one fierce push the orgasm he'd held just out of her reach now shattered her instantly. He locked still and deep, allowing her to ride the wave of it while fully anchored on his thick hardness. The pleasure of possessing him was so intense, all she could do was curl her nails into his back and scream.

'Oh, Emmy,' he growled with a satisfied glitter as he watched her go rigid and then crumble about him. 'You're so hot.'

She took a moment to catch her breath, stretching her legs wide to accommodate his size and giving her the leverage to push her hips up and into his—seeking to topple his self-control. 'How hot?' she murmured, daring him to lose it.

She traced his back with pleasure—discovering his strong, taut muscles again as they rippled with the strain he was putting them under as he surged into her again and again.

'More,' she breathed. Pure instinct driving her.

He swore, an earthy, crude celebration of their coming together and all it did was turn her on more. Her energy returned, with manifold intensity until finally they moved ferociously—pounding together in a fierce, passionate dance—pushing closer and closer, each driving action hurtling them both faster into that fantastic tumult of sensation—of white-hot, scalding satisfaction. She screamed it out until she could scream no more and all that fantastic tension snapped.

'We're damn good at this, Emmy,' Javier said a while later as he rested his head on his hand and watched her attempt to recover her breath. 'You do realise that, don't you?'

Sensations were still storming around her body—every drop of blood pulsed with the remnants of ecstasy. She didn't want to answer.

She didn't want reality to return. She wanted to remain suspended like this, as if in some dream state of pure bliss.

He chuckled. Her lack of response obviously cluing him in to her wrecked status.

He leaned close again. His kiss was luxuriant and indulgent—slow and lush, as if he had all the time in the world with which to savour and arouse her all over again.

But it didn't take long. As impossible as it was, her hunger returned, strong and powerful, and she shifted instinctively closer.

He met her gaze. His mouth curved. His body moved.

CHAPTER SEVEN

FOR ONLY THE second time in years, Emerald woke late. She stretched, taking the moment to appreciate the pure luxury of the wide bed and pure linen sheets and the delectable stiffness in intimate places.

'Sleeping beauty arises.' Javier grinned from the window as she sat up.

Emmy's heart skittered at his freshness in his bright white tee, black swim shorts and bare feet. His vitality was incredibly magnetic. 'Is Luke—?'

'Up and playing.' Javier lounged one hand against the back of the large armchair at the foot of the massive bed. 'He's had a very messy breakfast and is currently destroying the block towers Thomas's been building with him.'

She relaxed back against the plump pillows. 'That sounds good.'

'It's very good.' Javier inclined his head with

a satisfied expression. 'He's very happy. So you can rest a while longer if you need to.'

Something curled in her belly. She didn't want to *rest*. She wanted something else from Javier. Heat built in her cheeks as she realised the truth he'd stripped from her that first night. When it came to Javier Ramon Torres, Emerald was a wanton nymph who couldn't get enough of his kisses. But that madness had been last night. Now the day was bright and she wasn't sure what he wanted—if, indeed, he wanted anything.

'Though I have something for you.' Knowing amusement glinted in his eyes.

She stared as he straightened and held out the package she'd not realised he'd been hiding behind his back. It was gorgeously wrapped in black paper with a white ribbon. Yet her core temperature slipped a few notches. 'When did you get that?' she asked, awkwardness rising.

'The chopper brought it in with some other supplies this morning.'

'This morning?' How had she slept through the sound of the helicopter arriving *again*? The soundproofing in the cabins was astounding and it made her grateful for the monitor

Thomas had put into Luke's room even though he had taken the room on just the other side.

As she toyed with the wrapping, her skin chilled too. *This* wasn't what she wanted from Javier—not treats or rewards. She didn't want any things. *All* she actually wanted from him was his touch and even that she didn't *want* to want. 'You don't need to give me anything, Javier.'

He sighed and sat on the edge of the bed. 'Why don't you open it and see what it is? I ordered it after you gave me the book yesterday.'

'Before...'

'Before.' His gaze narrowed on her with mocking humour. 'So don't start thinking poisonous things. I'm not rewarding you because you let me have my wicked way with you again. Why don't you open it before you decide to reject it?'

That he guessed her fears so quickly made her feel ungrateful and overly cautious and appallingly judgy of him. Releasing a wary breath, she unwrapped the gift and discovered a digital camera in a large box.

'I can't accept this,' she murmured as she carefully pulled the camera from the packaging. It was so fancy she wasn't even sure how to turn it on. She set it down on the bed beside her and frowned up at him. 'Javier—'

'I want you to take more pictures of Luke and me. More of your aide-memoires. So it's for Luke as much as anything,' he said matter-of-factly. 'And for me.'

Stilled, she gazed at him. 'Oh, of course. I'd like to do that.'

She appreciated that this request was part of the forgiveness building between them, and part of his relationship building with Luke. And when he was older Luke would see that his father had been around and was there for him from a young age.

'Thank you,' he said.

She smiled wistfully. 'Stop acting so chivalrous. You know *I'm* the one who needs to say thank you.'

'Acting?' he echoed with a gleam in his eye. 'What makes you think I'm acting? Maybe I truly am chivalrous.' He waggled his brows. 'Anyway, I'm betting you want to get up and check in with Luke. Am I right?'

With a swallow she nodded and he left her to dress. Emmy's heart thudded heavily, as if drumming in impending doom. Javier had been right: last night had been inevitable. But *her* newly discovered, awkward truth was that last night hadn't been enough.

After breakfast she curled up on deck, reading the instruction booklet that came with the camera, and experimented with taking shots.

'Why are you taking photos of your hand?' Javier stretched out on the deck, moving toys in and out of Luke's reach.

'I'm experimenting with the light.'

He nodded and rolled to his stomach, looking lithe and gorgeous as he observed his mini-me. Emmy had to fiddle with the camera settings just to stop herself staring at the two of them.

'You've been on your own since you were how old?' Javier asked after a while.

'Sixteen.'

'And travelling the world all that time?'

'For seven years.'

'That's a long time.'

'And a lot of places.' She smiled in reminiscence. 'But I've been on the Galapagos for almost two years of that seven.'

'And how had you not fallen for some guy

in all that time?' He lifted his chin and scruti-
nised her. 'Was there no boyfriend ever?'

She shook her head.

'Girlfriend?'

She kept shaking her head.

'How, Emmy? You're a sensual woman.
You're...' He frowned slightly, as if picking
his words carefully. 'That night we met...'

Yes, she knew she'd not exactly made it difficult for him. At the time they hadn't discussed
it much, they'd been too carried away in the
intensity of the moment. She'd been so eager,
she knew her enthusiasm had swept away his
concern when he'd realised. And then his main
response to the discovery of her inexperience
had been determination to make it even better for her.

'I don't believe you never had any other opportunity before that night.' He moved another of Luke's toys. 'So why me—why then?
What happened to make you choose differently then?'

She didn't know what to say when the plain
truth was that *he* had happened. *He* was the
difference. It wasn't as if she'd decided one
day that the next man she met was going to be

the one; it had all been because of him—only because of him. He'd walked into her life and swept her away. He still swept her away. And if he'd walked into her life five years ago or five years from now, she was afraid he'd still have that same effect on her. He reached forward, rolling one of the toys in his hand, then squeezing it.

'I'm not going to feed your ego,' she finally answered with a teasing smile.

But he didn't laugh. 'Has there…?' He cleared his throat. 'Has there been anyone else since then?'

'I have a *baby*, Javier.' Droll amusement bubbled out of her. As if she'd had any time or inclination, given her circumstances. 'What do you think?'

He paused and his answer came slowly. 'I think I wouldn't blame you if you'd sought a momentary escape…'

Was that what he'd done since then? She stiffened at the stab of hurt inside. 'Well, I didn't.'

He was staring right into her eyes but he still didn't smile. 'Me neither.'

She stared back at him as an illicit heat slowly infiltrated her nether regions. She'd chosen not to think about the time they'd been apart. Why would she torture herself with the thought of all the women he'd had since that night with her? But to hear that there'd been *none*?

Now his lips twisted. 'That surprises you?'

'I don't know.' She shot him a look. '*You* weren't a virgin that night, Javier.'

Amusement crinkled around his eyes as he inclined his head in an admission. 'No, I wasn't.'

'So why not…?'

'Work,' he answered shortly.

She chuckled at his hasty retreat behind that remote expression he'd perfected. 'Don't worry. I won't take that admission to mean anything other than that you've been as busy as I have. Only you were doing other things, like building billions in the bank and beginning a boutique hotel empire. Just as I know you won't read anything into my not being intimate with anyone else since either.'

His eyes widened and he emitted a sound between a cough and a laugh. 'Emmy…'

'Relax, Javier, I get it. You're curious, but you don't want a long-term relationship with me.'

He had the grace to smile sheepishly but

there was a hint of remorse in his eyes that surprised her. 'With anyone, Emmy. Not just you.'

'No marriage?' she asked lightly, not really hoping for an answer given the barriers she expected him to raise any second now. 'Not ever? Why not?'

'I don't believe in it.'

'Really?' She maintained her airy tone and smile. 'As an institution? A construct of the society in which we live?'

He laughed. 'I just don't think it ever works out in anyone's best interests.'

'Not ever? You don't believe there's such a thing as happy ever after?'

He shrugged carelessly. 'I don't believe in fairy tales, no.'

'So you don't really believe there are dragons, either? There's not really any treasure to be found on an island? Okay, good to know.' She mirrored his shrug, only her carelessness was completely feigned.

She'd enjoyed that light, silly talk of dragons and magical creatures that night on the beach. And even though it had been a transient moment, it had meant something—long before she'd learned of Luke's existence within her. She'd been unable to forget Javier. And suddenly she couldn't fake anything any more, there was only plain truth and it slipped out of her in a sad little sigh. 'I haven't felt that chemistry with anyone else.'

For a moment he gazed back into her eyes, his own mix of cocoa and coffee dilating. 'Me neither.'

It was such a low mutter she wasn't sure she'd even heard him properly. She swallowed, trying to ease the sudden constriction in her throat. 'What do you think that means?'

He shook his head slowly and she felt that warning within at his withdrawal. 'Nothing other than what it is, Emmy. Strong chemistry. That's all.' He drew in a breath. 'And it will pass.'

She was sure he was right but there was a tiny fear, buried deep within like a seed about to sprout, that wondered if—for her at least—he was wrong.

'But I don't think it will go away until we deal with it properly,' he added.

And he wanted it to go away? Good, because so did she. It felt like vulnerability.

'And if we deal with it properly?' she asked. 'What happens then?'

'We move forward.' He shifted on the rug.

Her mouth dried as anticipation feathered goosebumps over her skin at the simple glimpse of him. Yes, getting rid of this distraction would make things easier as they worked out how they'd jointly care for Luke. They'd shake their future free from this lust. 'And dealing with it? You mean...like last night?'

'Mmm-hmm.' His eyes told her everything his words didn't.

'How long will it take, do you think?' she asked, shivering at the prospect.

His gaze lingered on her lips. 'I don't know,' he murmured huskily. 'But I'm willing if you are.'

It should have just been a flirty joke, but there was a raw element that chimed a low chord within her. The fact was they'd been drawn to each other on a purely physical level from the moment they'd met and it wasn't going to be exhausted all that quickly.

'We have a few days on board, right?' She looked at him with growing warmth. 'So...'

'We make the most of them?'

She nodded. It could be a huge risk but, given that she couldn't *think* when there was this sensual fog around her, she needed to clear her head to be able to hold her ground with him in the long run.

'So, have you had many girlfriends?' she asked even as she hated herself for her needy curiosity.

His eyes widened at the question.

'You asked me,' she pointed out with a little spirit. 'I don't think it's unfair to expect you to reciprocate.'

'You want full reciprocation?' Now there was a gleam in his eyes that made her think he wasn't thinking about sharing minor confidences, but other more physical things. 'Okay.' He smiled glibly. 'I had a girlfriend at university.'

She bit the edge of her lip because she wasn't sure how seriously he was taking this, but she wanted to ask more. 'Was she the reason why you dropped out?'

'As loath as I am to admit it, she was a big part of that decision.'

'What happened?'

He grimaced wryly. 'We were both extremely

driven to succeed—each with our own reasons why. But when it came to it, she didn't believe that I had what it took to get the success that she craved so badly.'

She hadn't believed in him? Emmy was surprised. 'What did she do?'

That teasing light faded from Javier's eyes and for a moment Emmy didn't think he was going to answer.

'She cheated to get ahead,' he said baldly.

'Cheated on exams? Or cheated on you?' She held her breath.

'As she slept with our professor, I'd say both.'

Emmy gaped, shocked. 'I'm sorry.' And she was—both sorry for what had happened and sorry for asking, because he clearly didn't like thinking about it, let alone answering any questions about it.

'I'm not, it was good.' He laughed but it had a bitter edge. 'I got my focus where I needed it to be—which was on work and on doing what I needed to do on my own. But I did have flings, Emmy. A number of nights…'

'But nothing serious?' Emmy muttered. That university girlfriend must have hurt him very

badly to put him off marriage so completely—
which meant he must've loved her a lot.

He shook his head.

'And what made you so driven to succeed?'
she asked, her heart aching a little.

He had that rare combination of ambition and
discipline and she suspected he was a complete
workaholic. She'd seen him snatching moments
every time Luke slept to work on his laptop or
phone. He was almost always 'on call' to respond to the chimes of incoming messages.

His eyes veiled and he shrugged. 'I just always was.'

She knew him well enough now to see that
those walls had gone right up again—she recognised that expression. And she also recognised his lie—something had happened. He
just didn't want to say what. But she let the
conversation slide despite her burgeoning
curiosity. Because if she asked anything too
personal, he might insist on the same from
her—especially now she'd been the one to insist on 'reciprocation'.

She had to retreat. There was no need for
them to open up too deeply. Not when he'd
just said their physical intensity would fade.

Once it did, then it would only be necessary for them to make amicable arrangements for sharing Luke's care.

So she swallowed back all the burning questions that filled her brain, on the heartache she feared might follow, and focused on what was right in front of her, right now.

'Will it fade slow or fast, do you think?' she pondered aloud, injecting that lightness back into herself with a cheeky giggle at her own thoughts. 'The chemistry, I mean. Either way, the best is done, now, right? It only goes downhill from here. Every time we're together, it will be a little less awesome than the last.'

'Huh?' He sat up and glared at her; his muscles actually jumped. 'Emerald Jones, that's fighting talk and you know it.'

'Do I?' She blinked at him.

He sat back on his heels. 'Is it time for Luke to have a nap?' Javier didn't even try to hide the sly look in his eyes.

Emmy laughed. 'Luke runs to *his* schedule, not ours.'

'Well...' Javier squeezed another toy in front of Luke's face and sat back as if he weren't at all concerned '...that's fine for now. I can wait.'

'Can you?' she teased, because those bunching muscles of his were telling another story.

'Don't doubt me, Emerald,' he said with downright menacing softness. 'I'll help you realise just how *far* from downhill certain things are about to go.'

CHAPTER EIGHT

'*WHY* ARE YOU awake?' Javier groaned as he watched Emmy slip from the bed and pull on her favourite—okay, *only*—linen dress. 'More to the point, *how* are you awake? We only fell asleep thirty seconds ago.' A slight exaggeration, but it was what it felt like.

'I want to capture the sunrise,' she whispered and came back to press a kiss to his lips. 'You stay here. I suspect Luke is awake anyway.'

'You should come back here and sleep in.' He was only beginning to appreciate how tired she'd been from caring for Luke on her own all these months.

'As if you're making that possible?'

He chuckled and went to tug her back into his arms, but she'd pulled away before he could stop her.

Javier closed his eyes and groaned. He'd unleashed, not a dragon, but a camera-loving demon. These days she caressed that tech more than she caressed him. He laughed inwardly at his jealousy of an inanimate object. And he couldn't get back to sleep now, not without her. That realisation sent a thread of unease down his spine.

What she did—or didn't do—shouldn't matter so much to him. It shouldn't impact on his mood or on his day or on his choices. He tapped his phone and the curtains slid back to reveal that pre-dawn glimmer of light, and he steeled himself to go into the office. There were multiple messages that needed answering, so he spent a few hours on the phone and laptop, exercising the self-control that he was suddenly determined to maintain. Because it could slip, he acknowledged. He could so easily spend all day kissing her. But he wasn't going to. And he wasn't going to listen hard for her voice, or look forward to lunch, or keep an eye on the door in case she went past...

Irritated beyond belief at his failure to *not* do any of those things for hours, he pulled on some swim shorts and went to find his son's mother in the middle of the afternoon.

Luke was napping and Thomas was re-arranging the toys and books Javier had ordered. Emmy was curled on the plush sofa. It was her favourite place in the shade, over-looking both the pool and the sea, but she was intently watching something on a tablet. She looked up guiltily as he stepped nearer.

'I hope you don't mind—your assistant said it was okay for me to use this.' She lifted the tablet. 'That it's a spare.'

'You can use anything on board, Emmy. You don't need to ask.' He sat down beside her. 'What are you watching?'

'How-to videos.'

'How to what?' He leaned a little closer to peer at the screen. 'Drive your man wild in bed?'

'Are you saying I need lessons?' she asked archly, but the hint of vulnerability in her eyes scratched a line of discomfort just beneath his skin.

'You know I'm not.' He laughed, leaning closer to steal a kiss. 'Photography skills?'

She nodded and smiled at him. 'That camera is amazing. I want to do it justice.'

'Or you could just have fun with it.' He shrugged, struggling to pull back from her.

'I want to use it properly. I enjoy it.'

That had been obvious in the photos she'd taken of Luke all these months—they showed her eye for framing a good picture. He was pleased he'd found something to give her that she couldn't refuse. Other than his body. He wanted to build more of a bridge between them; it was going to be important for Luke. And this was all about Luke, he reassured himself. He wanted his son to have the security he'd never had. To know that both parents wanted him, loved him, and would be there for him.

Javier watched the shiver ripple down her body as he stroked her arm. She was incredibly responsive to his touch and it spurred him to touch more. He'd discovered there was nothing better than torturing them both with tiny touches. He bent closer to blow softly across the sensitive skin between her shoulder blades. She turned towards him, her lips parted in pure invitation. It was exactly what he'd wanted and everything he couldn't resist.

Yet it still wasn't enough to satisfy the developing ache inside him.

For a few days there'd been nothing but that sensual magic between them as they'd submitted to the sweet, savage desire. And still his curiosity deepened. He didn't want it to deepen. He didn't want to think about her all the time like this. He wanted this all-consuming lust to ease. But it wasn't. Perhaps if he satisfied every element of his curiosity, then it might finally ebb.

He knew she was untrusting and wary of being judged. It seemed she suspected the worst and expected the worst—not just of him, but everyone. He wanted to know why. He wanted her to trust him enough to tell him why.

He knew how hard she'd worked, and he knew better than anyone how inexperienced she really was with men—seemingly with *all* relationships—so what was it that caused her reticence and resentment? Why had she not had a real home for so long? Who had judged her so much? How and why? What had she done—or not done—to deserve it? He needed to know more.

She wasn't this untrusting purely because of him. Sure, he'd been selfish in not telling her his real name that night. And when she'd found out who he was and that he'd invested in Lucero's property, she'd been angry and resentful. But there was real fear within her too. Real fear that he might have taken Luke away from her. He had the horrible feeling she still worried that might happen and he hated that idea. So what was it that had been taken from her in the past? There had to have been loss. Was that why she'd not returned to her homeland in all this time?

He really didn't like the thought of her being hurt that badly.

They couldn't move forward without building some level of trust. Somehow he needed to get her to talk to him about more than her travels, her work. They'd conversed for hours about her voluntary work and the eco-action the Flores Foundation had undertaken to make the former hostel sustainable. He'd known about some from Lucero, of course, but getting the detail from her was fascinating and highly relevant to his own future plans.

But learning more about Emerald *herself* was almost impossible. Tempted as he was, he couldn't go behind her back to discover more about her. But using only his hands to open the puzzle box that was Emerald Jones wasn't working. He was going to use his mouth in more than one way too.

Maybe if he offered her real security she'd open up. That was one thing he'd felt short of when he was younger and being shoved from boarding school to 'guest bedroom' and back again. But getting his first apartment building had helped and, as far as he could tell, Emmy hadn't had a permanent home in a long time. Maybe she'd like that?

'You know, we can't stay here for ever,' he said idly. 'I'm mostly based in New York. My apartment is in a nice location. There's no reason why I can't buy another in the same building for you.'

He watched closely for her response. She paled fractionally and he saw her struggle to swallow.

'I can't afford an apartment in New York,' she said firmly. 'And I'm not going to let you buy one for me.'

Yeah, he'd known she'd instantly reject the idea of him housing her. She still didn't want to accept anything of consequence from him. But he smiled smugly. 'Well, if you won't let me buy you an apartment, then you'll have to move into mine.'

She stilled. 'I'll live wherever you want me to for the next eighteen months.'

He wasn't rising to her throwing that damn stupid demand in his face this time. 'It makes most sense,' he mulled. 'It'll be more convenient.'

'Convenient for what?' she asked, too calmly.

'It'll give us both best access to Luke and it will be less confusing for him.'

'Confusing? He's nine months old, I don't think he's going to notice where I'm sleeping.'

That she was thinking about where she was sleeping tickled him. 'We'll come back to the islands often though,' he added. 'I want him to understand his heritage more than I ever got to. He needs to know where he comes from.'

She turned to face him. 'You didn't get that?'

He saw the curiosity burning in her eyes and steeled himself to answer at least a couple of the questions he knew she was bound to ask. 'My father left when I was young and I learned nothing of him or his family other than his nationality. I taught myself Spanish as a teenager.' He glanced at her and referred back to their son as quickly as he could. 'I'm glad you use some with Luke.'

She nibbled her lip. 'I'm not great at it, but Connie helped me.'

Javier nodded. 'You know Thomas is fluent.'

'Of course,' she chuckled. 'That's good.'

Javier nodded. 'Usually I have to travel a bit,' he said cautiously. 'I thought you and Luke would travel with me.'

'You want me to travel with you as well?' Her eyes widened.

'I think that's what's best for Luke, don't you?'

Emmy nodded and swallowed back the massive lump in her throat. Of course, it was always about Luke. Javier seemed very keen for their son to have both parents around. Given she'd just learned his father hadn't been there for him, she was beginning to understand why, and she wanted to understand so much more. 'If that's what you think is best.'

'I do, but what do you think?' He watched her, his expressionless game face back on.

'These are your eighteen months,' she reiterated quietly. 'You get to call the shots.'

And if he wasn't going to give much away, she wasn't sure she wanted to either.

He looked at her. As he slowly shook his head and turned away she knew she'd disappointed him somehow.

Later that afternoon, Emmy watched Javier splash with Luke at the bottom of the stairs at the very back of the boat. The sea was a gorgeous temperature and a stunning blue. The island behind them was a perfect backdrop. Emmy lay on the step just above the water line, her camera strap looped around her neck as she watched the two of them splashing through the viewfinder. Luke giggled as Javier teased him. The baby was at ease now—as was Javier in holding and reaching for him. Emmy played with varying settings to capture every moment because they were so magic.

'Oh,' she breathed and smiled. 'I just took the best photo ever.'

'Hmmm?' Carrying Luke, Javier splashed back up the stairs and she turned the camera so he could see the display on the back.

'You had someone photo-bombing you.' She laughed.

Luke and Javier were smiling at each other,

the droplets of water sparkling on their bronzed skin. But in the background was a Galapagos tortoise in the water, his head up, looking as if he was smiling. And beyond him gleamed a snippet of the golden sand of the uninhabited island behind.

'You're right, that's an amazing shot.' Javier glanced up at her. 'Forward it to me?'

'Of course.' She sat back.

She more than liked it. She couldn't stop staring at it. The two most handsome males on the planet—both better looking than any model.

'Put the camera down and join us,' Javier said roughly.

Emmy's heart melted at the invitation and she quickly put the camera away before going to sit on the step beside him. His arm rested across Luke's little belly as they dangled their feet in the water and gazed at the tortoises on the island, who gazed with equal curiosity right back.

'They're just incredible, aren't they?' Javier murmured.

'I never get sick of staring at them. The islands are so remote, so isolated, all the creatures have evolved into something completely unique. So precious, they're fascinating.'

'And beautiful.'

'And undamaged by the rest of the world.' She pondered the rarity before her. 'So lucky.'

She felt him turn his head. 'The rest of the world damaged you?'

'That's what *people* do, isn't it?' she asked lightly.

'And that's why you avoid them now?'

'I don't avoid them.' She scoffed at the suggestion. 'I just choose to live in paradise.'

'This is your definition of paradise?'

'Yes.' She nodded.

'Somewhere remote and isolated and unique?' He echoed her words. 'Like the end of the world or something. Somewhere away from everyone, everything else.' He paused. 'And a place where people don't tend to stay. Visitors come and go. There are no connections for long.'

She stilled at the serious edge to his tone. 'I take it you disagree?'

'I think it's somewhere *safe*.'

'Maybe.' She forced a smile. 'Or maybe you're overthinking it.'

'Or maybe you've just got a little prickly because I've got too close to the truth.' He cocked his head. 'Maybe you're avoiding *life*, Emmy.'

'How do you figure that, really?' She nudged his shoulder and added an eye roll for good measure. 'I have a child—I've been raising him on my own.'

'But that's the point. You've deliberately isolated yourself. And yes, thank goodness for Lucero and Connie for being there to help you to the extent that you'd allow anyone to help you.'

She stared at him.

'There's a compelling difference between you and the Galapagos creatures, though,' he mused quietly. '*They're* not afraid of people. They've not had the predatory experiences that we've had. They've not built the defences—'

'You're looking at a giant tortoise,' she interrupted with a pointed wave of her hand. 'What do you think that shell is for?'

'It's his portable house.' Javier laughed at her. 'Like a little caravan, he has his own roof over his head. But they're friendly, Emmy. That's my point. They're not afraid of people.'

'And I am? Is that what you're ever so unsubtly trying to suggest?'

'Maybe, yes. I think you've got a bit afraid of the rest of the world. I think you've been using your situation with Luke to avoid re-entering a full life.'

'You don't think my life is full?'

'I think it's lonely,' he said quietly. 'I think you've been lonely for a while.'

'And you think that's why I let you seduce me so easily that night?' She felt her defensiveness grow. She wanted Luke to be enough. For her to be enough for him. 'Is *your* life full?' she challenged.

'I'm realising that perhaps it's not, no. I know I focus on work to the detriment of other aspects of my life.' He sighed. 'Certainly recently, I've not...'

'Not what?'

'Taken time for me.'

'Is that what this is now?'

'Partly, perhaps.' Javier reached for her camera and fiddled with it. 'Can we get a selfie with this?'

With dexterity he cuddled Luke and leaned close to her and somehow took a shot. With their wet hair, sun-kissed skin and huge smiles, anyone else looking at it would see a perfect family shot. But the image hurt Emmy's heart—because it wasn't real. They weren't a true family and she was sure he'd only taken the photo as a means to end that conversation.

Yet the moment had been real enough. There'd been pure joy in that instant. But it was only an instant. A permanent reminder of a temporary pleasure. An emotion that wasn't sustainable and that had no real depth behind it.

'That's a good one,' he said.

'You can see the likeness between you and Luke. The resemblance is strong.'

Javier studied the shots. What she said was true. 'I've never looked much like anyone else in my family.'

'Not your father?'

He hesitated. He never discussed his parents, but Emerald wasn't just anyone any more. She was someone he wanted to trust and have trust him. So he answered as briefly as he could. 'I have few memories of him. No pictures. He walked out when I was a child. I thought he'd come back one day and take me with him.

But he didn't.' He glanced at her. 'I don't want Luke ever to feel that.'

'That?'

'Being left behind. Being rejected. All that good stuff that sears the soul of a five-year-old, you know.' His lips twisted and his tone was dry as he tried to make light of it, but it wasn't remotely funny.

'Javier—'

'My mother remarried,' he said crisply, finishing the story on his own terms before she could ask him details he didn't want ever to recall. 'She wanted a real family with him. They had two sons. Jacob and Joshua.' He shot her a look and chuckled. 'I didn't quite fit with that, did I?'

But Emmy didn't laugh with him; she looked deeply troubled. 'What happened to you when she remarried?'

He grimaced, absently fiddling with the clasp of his watch. 'I was sent to very good boarding schools. But despite their often-quoted massive investment in me and the stellar grades I delivered, it turned out my stepfather had no intention of bringing me into the fold of the family business. Because I was never part of *his* family.'

Emerald looked pensive. 'What was his business?'

He almost laughed; the question she'd asked wasn't anything as intrusive as he'd feared. 'Car-parking buildings.'

Emmy stared at him fixedly for a second and he could see her trying not to smile.

'I know, super sexy, right?' He shook his head. 'But he made millions. And all I wanted to do was build a business with an even bigger and better bottom line. And one that was a damn sight sexier than car parking.'

'Financing is sexy?'

'You don't think so?'

She wrinkled her nose. 'I thought you were a surfer.'

'I can surf and finance,' he teased, easing into the detail of his work. That was where he'd found his calling. 'Multi-talented, I am.' He chuckled. 'But you realise that first up I needed money. Not going to lie, I needed the capital first and the freedom. So I crashed out of my studies, did the trading and investing and worked around the clock for years. And when I got enough I began investing in other things. Other companies and—'

'Property.' She nodded. 'Some hotels. Sustainable. Well designed. So now you have...'

'Several property investments in various places and I travel between them all.'

'And that includes here.' She frowned. 'When it's almost impossible to invest here.'

'I'm able to do that through my father.' He shrugged. 'That's the one thing he gave me, I guess. Even if he hadn't intended to leave me with anything.'

At the look she shot him, he regretted mentioning him again.

'You don't know why he left?' she asked quietly.

He braced, not at the question, but the gaping void of his own answer, and just shook his head. Javier couldn't either forget or forgive his father, even though he'd tried to do both.

Emmy frowned. 'Had they been unhappy for a while?' she asked.

'She'd met someone else,' he said briefly.

'The man she later married?' Emmy watched as he grimaced, nodded, and the blue in her eyes deepened with concern. 'Maybe he thought you'd have more security with her if he wasn't around? Maybe he did what he thought was best for you both?'

And maybe Javier couldn't bear to think about it because it wasn't something he could ever know. His mother had avoided any discussion of his father from the moment he'd vanished. Javier had only learned where his father had gone and what had happened to him a few years ago. But the reason why he'd left—so abruptly and so finally? That he could never truly know.

'Anyway, I wanted a foothold here and now I've got it.' He sighed. 'Somewhere where I might belong.' He instantly regretted that last slipping out because he saw her expression turn even more caring.

'You don't feel as if you belong anywhere?' she asked.

He couldn't answer honestly—only flip it back on her and try to lighten it. 'Do you?'

'I feel at home in the water,' she said softly. 'I always have.'

He smiled at that. 'Like a redheaded siren.'

'Dragon, a sea dragon,' she corrected with a tilt of her head. 'Have things improved with your mother and stepfather since you've become more successful than the car-parking empire?'

Yeah, he was so done with this conversation. 'There's honestly little but the remnants of festering resentment on both sides,' he drawled through the painful truth. 'I don't bother with family occasions. It's not worth the awkwardness.'

'Perhaps it's not too late for a reconciliation?' She looked so hopeful it almost hurt to answer her honestly.

'No.' He shook his head and half smiled at her naiveté. 'There aren't neatly tied threads and happy endings in life, Emmy. There's just the next phase. It'll have good things and bad, the one true constant is that it will change.'

'So, in your world nothing lasts?'

'In *any* world, nothing ever does.'

'And yet you like to build your beautiful hotels and take care of the environment around them.'

Emmy's eyes were very blue and very steady and as he looked into them Javier's chest tightened painfully.

'Things can last a good while though, right?'

she said quietly. 'Like the stars and the moon and the sun. Some things can last long enough.'

He laughed, somehow soothed by her words and the sweet promise of a child's nursery rhyme.

'Some things can last a lifetime.' She seemed to gaze right into his soul. 'Couldn't that be long enough?'

CHAPTER NINE

EMMY WAITED BUT Javier didn't reply. That he'd ever felt unwanted stunned her. 'I'm sorry your parents didn't love you the way they should have.' He should have been utterly adored and she couldn't believe he hadn't been. So no wonder he was protective of Luke.

'It's okay, Emmy,' he said dismissively even as he gazed at her intently. 'I know my worth.'

Did he? Or did he think it was only because of his bank balance? Was that why he was so driven in his business? Why he was so guarded? Because even now he'd barely told her anything and she just *knew* there was more to it. That there was so much more he'd avoided telling her by his swift segue into his work story. She suspected he used work to avoid a lot of things.

As she breathed in, trying to frame her thoughts, he leaned close and pressed a kiss to her mouth. 'But I'm not sure you know yours.'

She shook her head, trying to remain clear-headed and not let him distract her with his seduction. But everything inside her seemed to have softened and she wanted not just to understand him, but for him to understand her. And suddenly she realised the longer she remained reticent, the worse it would be when he learned the truth. And he would find out eventually, somehow. He'd probably make it his business in the end. Shame crawled over her in a prickling heat with embarrassment and resentment at the thought of some stranger picking over the pitiful facts of her life and telling him behind her back. The fewer people who knew, the better—for Luke's sake as much as anything. So she needed to explain it to Javier herself.

'I know my worth,' she muttered sadly. 'And it's not what it should be.'

He leaned back and studied her sombrely. 'Why do you say that?'

'I don't come from a good family,' she confessed.

'No? What do you mean by good?' He offered an encouraging smile. 'There's no such thing as a perfect family.'

'A law-abiding, honest one would be a start.'

His eyebrows lifted.

'It was petty crime…theft, cars, tech gear, drugs. They're small time but persistent and unhappily married and I have an older brother, Sterling.' She swallowed and gave into the desperate temptation to confide in him completely. 'We were at different schools.' She smiled sadly. 'I'd got a scholarship. You're looking at a former state champion water-polo player.'

'Wow.' He slung his arm across her shoulder and squeezed. 'Go you.'

For just a moment she rested her head on his shoulder. 'My family disagreed. They said school was a waste of time. That I should be less uppity and do the work they needed me to do.'

'And what work was that?'

She pulled away from him and he dropped his arm. 'Sterling had been selling drugs at the school gate.' She stared down at the camera, absently holding it closer. 'I took the fall for him.'

He watched her carefully. 'Why was that?'

'I had to.' She licked her lips, but her mouth remained dry and her throat almost painfully tight. 'He was on his final strike…if he was caught again he was going to prison. My parents said I had to...' She trailed off, hating the horror from that time.

The emotional manipulation had been severe.

'So you said it was you.' He finished it for her with a nod. 'Then what happened?'

'I'd hoped my teachers would see through me. That they'd know I was lying, trying to protect my brother.' She licked her lips again. 'I know it was wrong to lie. It's *always* wrong to lie.'

'It must've been damn hard to make those choices when you're wanting to protect someone you love.'

She nodded, swallowing awkwardly.

'And please your parents.'

She chewed the inside of her cheek, unable to answer.

'I'm guessing your teachers didn't pick up on the truth,' he said softly.

'I guess I convinced them.' But it had hurt. They'd known her for a couple of years. She'd always turned up, she'd always done her best, she'd never let them down. Yet all her past actions had counted for nothing in the face of a few words. Her family history—that assumption—had been used against her. It was as if they'd been waiting for her family blood to seep out. Waiting for her to mess up. Nothing she'd done prior had mattered, in their eyes her downfall was simply inevitable. Just a matter of time. They were so quick to believe the worst, not bothering to try to pick holes in her stupidly flimsy story.

'It was a good school.' She drew a breath. 'I'd worked so hard to get there. I had a part-time job at a fast-food place so I could buy my uniform and supplies and scrape together the travel money for the tournaments...' She swallowed. 'It was my first offence so the police let me off with a warning and some community service. But the principal kicked me off the water-polo team and expelled me from school.'

He waited quietly.

'My brother went to prison less than a month later. He was caught on a breaking and entering job.' She drew breath. 'So my "sacrifice" was all for nothing.'

Javier was very serious. 'And your parents?'

'Didn't care. They were never bothered about my schooling. They wanted me to take on the deliveries he could no longer do. They thought it was good timing that I'd been kicked out.' She lifted her head and stared across the clear water, unable to look at his reaction. 'I knew the only thing to do was leave. I needed a fresh start. I travelled around Australia, working in various cafés, then I went to hotels because often I'd get accommodation thrown in. I'd spend a few months and then move on until I'd saved enough for my passport and a one-way ticket abroad. I've been working or volunteering and travelling ever since.'

'Have you been back home at all?'

'It's no longer my home.' She shrugged. 'And now I have Luke I'd never go back. I don't want him near my family. I can't trust them.'

'You can't trust anyone?' he asked softly.

Silently she looked at him, her throat so constricted an answer was impossible.

'You know you can trust me, Emmy.'

Her heart ached because she really wished that were the case, but it wasn't. At some point he would judge her. It wasn't his fault, it was human nature. People always did. And she *had* screwed up, hadn't she?

'I'm sorry they all let you down. Your family, your school, your friends. That sucked, Emmy.'

'Car-parking buildings don't seem so bad now, right?' she tried to joke. 'My family business is way worse.'

'Oh…maybe.' He hugged her close and kissed her forehead. 'I'm glad you told me.'

'When I found out I was pregnant…' she murmured softly, releasing the burden of her deepest secrets to him, 'I thought about all my options. I didn't even know your full name. I didn't have any savings and I didn't even have paid employment. No family support. My only friend was an octogenarian on his death bed. What was I doing bringing a baby into that uncertainty? It was nothing short of reckless. But I wanted him for *me*. I wanted someone to love and to love me too. And that was immature and selfish of me because I wasn't in the best place to provide for him and I knew that. So when I found out who you really were? I was afraid you'd go for custody and, with your resources, you'd win easily and you'd be right to.'

She paused, afraid at how vulnerable she'd just allowed herself to be.

But he regarded her steadily and shook his head. 'That never would have happened,

Emmy. No judge would have taken him from you. You've given him more than I ever could—love, for one thing. The desire to do whatever is best for him—putting him first and yourself second.' He gazed at her. 'And I would never take him from you. You know, I never thought I wanted children. Ever. But I'm glad he's here.'

She leaned against him. 'I'm glad too.'

And as he lifted her chin and pressed a kiss to her mouth, her last thought—while she could still think—was that perhaps, just perhaps, things were going to be all right.

'I have an event I have to go to in Quito,' Javier said as he left the bed. 'I'd like you to come with me.'

Emmy tensed and lifted her head from the pillow. 'What kind of event?'

'It's business,' he said calmly, but he was watching her too intently with an amused look in his eyes.

'Why do I need to go?'

'You're the mother of my child—the sooner that little fact is out in the world, the better.'

'Why does anyone need to know?'

'I won't have Luke kept a secret. I don't want him to feel that I'm ashamed of him. We show a united front, Emmy. You're the mother of my son and we're friends.'

She swallowed the little hit at that descriptor. 'It just seems a little soon.'

'It's been over nine months already,' he reminded her wryly.

'Won't people be curious? You're wealthy... people are interested in you. They might ask about me, which would be bad.' She swallowed as he looked distinctly unfazed. 'People finding out about my background doesn't worry you?'

'Not in the least,' he said simply.

'You really don't care?'

'I really don't give a damn.' He watched her. 'Why would anyone think any less of you, just because of your family?'

She stared at him. 'They have before.'

'Then they weren't kind people. But you're still reluctant?' He bent over her and cupped her jaw and whispered against her skin. 'Don't you want to accompany me?'

'Are you trying to seduce me into saying yes?' she muttered.

As he pulled back she saw the teasing smile in his eyes. 'Isn't that better than threatening you?'

'I'm not sure.' She wasn't sure that that light teasing wasn't a form of torture all of its own. Because while it was blissful, she was beginning to fear there was nothing real behind it for him. Whereas for her? Something else was brewing. 'Is that what comes next if I say no?'

His amusement faded. 'Do you really think I'd try to order you, Emmy? That I insist on it as part of this eighteen-months thing?' He frowned and a hint of chagrin tightened his gaze. 'I'm actually not that guy. You think I'd leverage some kind of power over you? What would be the joy for me in that?' He shook his head. 'I don't get off on a power trip over you, I get off on *you*.'

Her heart seized, but she still couldn't answer. And that fear—that this was truly, purely physical for him—bloomed.

'Look, if you really don't want to, then I'll accept your answer and go alone.' He gazed at her and suddenly she was wary of the hint of coolness encroaching in his eyes and sensed him starting to withdraw.

She didn't want to lose the fragile intimacy that had built between them yesterday. And suddenly she couldn't say no. She was half afraid that she couldn't say no to him about anything. 'When is it?'

'Tomorrow night.'

'Tomorrow?' she choked. 'You can't be serious. I don't have—'

'Anything to wear? I can arrange—'

'No. *No*, Javier.'

'You can borrow it for the night and give it back to me the second we're home.' He waggled his eyebrows.

'Javier—'

'Let me buy you a damn dress, Emerald.'

'You're not spending stupid money on a dress I'll wear only once.'

'I won't spend stupid money and you can wear it more than once,' he growled. 'Wear it all the time.'

It was impossible not to smile at him. 'Why are you suddenly angry?'

'Because you refuse *anything* I offer.'

She laughed. 'That's *not* true. I've been living with you for the past week. Eating your food. Drinking your water. Learning how to use the camera you gave me. Sleeping in your *bed*. Everything. I've taken *everything*.'

'Not everything, barely the necessities.'

'Necessities?' She waved a hand around the yacht. *'Barely?'*

'You know what I mean.' He glared at her. 'You can't live your life in servitude to your son. You need things of your own as well. Your own life. You're a people person. You're good with them, you like them. You need to let more of them in your life.'

Her eyes widened. Maybe he was right, but somehow that truth saddened her.

'I want you to be happy,' he grumped. 'I want you to meet new people and make friends. Not be alone.'

She was shocked by his vehemence. 'I am happy. I'm *not* alone. I have Luke.'

'He can't even talk back, Emmy.'

'Not yet. But he's getting very close, you know. He can already say mama.'

Emmy shifted uncomfortably as she read the seriousness in Javier's expression. He was being thoughtful and kind, yet stupidly it hurt.

Because she wouldn't want or need anyone else if she had Javier, not just as her temporary lover, but as her best friend and mate for life.

But *he* didn't want that from *her*, did he? That was everything he *wasn't* offering.

CHAPTER TEN

EVEN THOUGH SHE'D accepted his invitation, Javier couldn't relax. There was a fleeting quality that made him uneasy—it wasn't just the too rapid sliding of their days on board. It was that the promise they'd made to liberate themselves of this damn chemistry couldn't be fulfilled. Because it wasn't easing. Not yet. So much for the 'downhill slide' she'd predicted. And worse, he had the growing apprehension that Emmy herself was like a mirage—a sylph who'd disappear if he turned his back too long and he'd be left again with this damned raging ache for her. And that if he went alone tonight, he couldn't quite trust she and Luke would still be here when he returned. He hated feeling as if something were about to slip through his fingers.

Because he'd felt it before. He'd come downstairs and the most important person in his life had been missing, never to return. And then he'd been tipped out of his home himself. And he hated even suspecting that he was at risk of something like that happening again.

It was because of Luke, wasn't it? The baby was so vulnerable and so precious...

But he assured himself Emmy wouldn't take him away. Not now he understood her a little more. She thought she needed to be needed and that she needed to *earn* her place—her respect—in people's lives. To earn her place in the world—all those years doing voluntary work? Was she trying to make up for her family's failings? Of course, it was far more complicated than that, but he knew her desire to work so hard for Connie was part of it. The same with Lucero. She'd poured everything into doing the best she could for both of them. And then in being the best mother possible to Luke—even when alone and exhausted. She tried to do her best. So she wasn't about to take her son from what Javier could give him.

But Javier didn't want her to do that with him. To work super hard at being the best possible...what? *Lover?*

She already was that. She didn't need to prove anything to him. And the last thing he wanted was for her to be with him out of any sense of *obligation*. He wanted her with him that way only because she wanted to be—only because she still felt that chemistry the way he did. Because that was all this was and he could still control it, couldn't he? He could spend the day locked in his office, taking time only to see Luke and not needing to set eyes on Emmy for hours. Surely he could do that.

Emmy smoothed the skirt of her dress, appreciating the silk beneath her fingers. It was her first evening out in eons. A snippet of her own time to act like an adult, not a maid, not a mother—but a woman. A whole person—one who'd even had the leisure time to be pampered beforehand to dress up. A beautician had been flown on board and it turned out there was a spa room below deck with a massage table and sauna and she'd very much enjoyed those facilities today.

Her lips felt slick from the rub of colour and her hair was completely loose for once, the curls enhanced—she didn't know how the stylist had worked her magic, but they weren't the usual tumbling tangle of strawberry red, they were actually ringlets.

But suddenly she was nervous. She'd not seen Javier for what felt like years. He'd been in the office, the door sealed shut for hours and now she wondered if she was suitably dressed for this wretched event.

'I can't believe there's a massage and treatment room on board the yacht,' she said dryly to cover her nerves as she walked to where he was waiting.

Javier gaped at her—from her hair, to her eyes, her mouth, her breasts and the flare of her hips, then he visibly hauled his wits together. 'You should definitely wear that dress again,' his voice rasped. 'Like, all the time.'

Yes? Well, he ought to wear suits that sharply tailored as well. She stared at him, drinking in his strong frame, and all that sensual awareness rose and tightened to the point where she couldn't breathe. So much for the chemistry *fading*.

'If we're going to get there at all, we'd better leave now.' Javier swiftly turned on his heel.

But Emmy's nerves fluttered as she strapped herself into the helicopter. She'd never left

Luke for more than an hour. And to be flying away and leaving him on a boat in the middle of the sea?

'Stop fretting, he'll be fine,' Javier murmured.

'I know he'll be fine. It's whether *I'll* be fine.'

'I'll do my best to distract you this evening.'

'I thought my mission was to meet new people and make new friends,' she teased archly.

'We can meet people *together.*' He sent her a dark glance that dipped again to her creamy cleavage.

Was that a possessive moment from him? She laughed but she felt it too. In fact she didn't want him talking alone to any other woman. *Ever.*

As the helicopter ascended, she stared down at the superyacht growing more distant by the second.

'Don't worry.' He took hold of her hand. 'We'll fly back for the night. It's only a couple of hours that we're away.'

She laced her fingers through his and squeezed, appreciating that reassurance. 'Thank you.'

He didn't release her hand for the entire

flight. He held it again as he walked with her into the banquet hall where the reception was being held. And he was open about their relationship the moment they met the chair of the gala committee on the receiving line.

'Emmy's the mother of my son.'

That was her status. Not his girlfriend. Never to be his wife, but the mother of his son. She knew he meant it respectfully but somehow it hurt, the words wearing a little hole in her heart—the fabric unravelling bit by bit, getting wider with every repetition as he introduced her to other guests. Yet she was proud to be Luke's mother and funnily enough she found she didn't mind the resultant staring of some of the guests. It was refreshing to be somewhere different and she'd dealt with all sorts in her travels. There was little she hadn't encountered and she could manage small talk. All that was involved was asking questions.

In the large reception room she noticed stunning pictures on the walls, promoting the Galapagos. Some of the images were outstanding. Halfway down the length of the vast room, she paused as she caught a glimpse of a familiar smile. That was the picture of Javier, Luke and the tortoise. *Her* picture—massively enlarged and looking gorgeous in the centre of the room.

'I hope you don't mind. I thought it would be a good one to use,' Javier murmured.

As she stared up at it, she noticed a small logo had been added to the bottom left of the print. *Emerald.*

'Do you mind?' he added after a moment.

'Of course not, it looks amazing.' She was bowled over. 'Thanks for the credit.'

'You deserve it. I've actually been approached by a couple of people who want to buy the rights to it.'

'Seriously?' Emmy was amazed. People were offering money to use her photo?

'Do you mind giving me exclusive rights, though?' He turned to face her. 'You'll be recompensed accordingly.'

'*You're* in the picture, Javier.' She laughed as she shook her head. 'And it's a holiday snap, I don't need anything for it.'

'Wrong answer,' he murmured. 'You really need to learn your value, Emmy.'

As they mingled, other guests commented once they learned she'd taken the shot that had become the favourite of the display.

'We have a lot of stunning shots taken on the islands, but that was an extraordinary moment to capture,' one woman said to her.

'I was very lucky.' Feeling a fraud, she smiled. 'Of course, it helps that I'm completely in love with my subject.' Emmy glanced again at the photo. The two males were in such sharp focus—one very young, one very virile. But *both* had her heart.

Her smile slipped as she realised the true extent of her vulnerability. They really did have her. She cared about Javier in a way he didn't and wouldn't ever want. Knowing something of his background, she understood why. His parents had been unhappy and she guessed he'd had a desperately insecure childhood, being sent away. He didn't trust people any more than she did, but then they differed: while she'd focused on building her tiny surprise family—of Luke—he'd focused on building his life through his work. And he was still focused on that, wasn't he? He didn't want more. He still retreated behind those walls when conversations veered fractionally too close to the personal, or distracted her with a joke or a kiss… He'd told her the merest of details and clearly had no intention of delving deeper or opening up to her more. But she wanted. So. Much. More.

So how on earth was she going to survive the next eighteen months? How was she to live the rest of her life connected and close to Javier, but not in the way she truly wanted?

'I'd love to be in a photo like that,' the woman continued. 'Most of us would.'

Emmy smiled. 'Yes, I took lots of pictures for passing tourists when I was out on the beaches.'

'No reason why you shouldn't get paid for that,' Javier chimed in softly.

'For doing someone a favour?' She turned and laughed at him.

'No, for giving someone a stunning piece of art.' He contemplated her seriously. 'When our hotel opens, lots of our guests would like beautiful pictures of them on the islands. You could take them.'

She paused. Had he said '*our*' hotel?

'You have talent,' he said, and she recognised he was going into his sell mode. 'You have skills and you have the interest and passion to develop those skills further. Why wouldn't you?'

Yes, Emmy wanted a job and for it to be something she could be proud of. But she didn't want to work for Javier. She *needed* independence—now more than ever. And she definitely didn't want to benefit from nepotism or charity.

'Emerald,' he said with soft warning and that suffering but amused look in his eyes as he watched the thoughts cross her face. 'You don't like people jumping to conclusions about you, yet you do it to me all the time...'

She paused and gave him a rueful smile. 'But you don't really need a photographer—'

'Don't I? I think it would be an added-value extra for our customers. You'd go on the boat tours with them, take the pictures.' He leaned back thoughtfully. 'In fact, I'm going to have to hire more than one.'

'Well, not me,' she said. 'I can't—'

'Accept any help?' He interrupted with raised eyebrows. 'Why be so determined not to accept any help, any advice, or make use of any contacts?'

'Because I want to make something of myself, *myself.* You of all people must understand that. No car-parking buildings, remember? You wanted to do your own thing. Prove to them that you could.'

'But you've *already* made something of yourself. You've dedicated years to voluntary work. You don't need to prove anything to anyone, Emmy. Not me. And not to yourself.' He huffed a breath. 'Why not do something you'd thrive on and love?'

'Look, it's a good idea,' she admitted. 'A lot of your guests would love it…but I can't be that person.'

He grabbed her hand and stopped her from walking away. 'Don't you think you deserve it?'

She looked at him questioningly.

'Help from someone? Support from someone? *Anything* from someone?'

'It's not that,' she murmured. She'd accepted help before. The problem was that she'd just realised what it was she did want from him. And it wasn't help or support. It was *everything.*

And that included her being able to offer support to him.

His grip on her tightened fractionally before

he suddenly released her and stepped back. 'Because it would be for me?'

She said nothing as another guest stepped up to speak to them, but she felt Javier's withdrawal and that ache in her heart intensified.

The evening slipped by in concerted effort of smiles and conversation. Emerald talked and focused so hard, anything to distract herself from her own realisation and that moment with Javier.

So she was tired when they returned to the helicopter and flew fast and low across the water to the waiting yacht. She dozed for most of the trip, her head resting on his shoulder, her hand held in his. Because despite her realisation, she couldn't deny herself his touch.

He gently roused her, then with a laugh half carried her from the 'copter onto the deck and towards his cabin.

'I need to check Luke,' she said softly, properly coming awake.

'I know,' he murmured. 'Already on it.'

The door to their baby's room was ajar. A square of light illuminated the room enough for her to see Luke in his cot. Her son seemed to have inherited her ability to sleep through

NATALIE ANDERSON213

the sound of a helicopter arriving. Her heart rose into her throat. He was so beautiful.

'I watch him when he's sleeping. I stare at him and I can't believe he's mine,' she confessed in a whisper. 'He's so perfect. It's like magic. And there's nothing I won't do to protect him.' She glanced up at Javier. 'Do you know what I mean?'

In the half-darkness she couldn't tell if he smiled back at her. But she heard the rasp in his whisper.

'I know exactly what you mean.'

That soft answer soothed her anxiety. Javier, she was certain, had fallen in love with Luke. And suddenly, in this midnight hour, having seen Luke, being with Javier...it made her wonder if magic might be real after all. Her heart filled with a bubble of hope. Maybe they just needed more time?

She'd told Javier her truth and he'd still wanted her to come with him tonight. Her family background didn't bother him. So then maybe, *maybe* this could work? Maybe, in time, he would open up to her fully? He would let her really know what it was that had kept him distanced for so long?

Yes, *she* was vulnerable, but she and Javier shared a bond—Luke—and they shared passion. They shared laughter too. Perhaps, in time, something more could grow from those foundations?

'Why are you smiling?' Javier asked when she'd led the way back up to his private deck.

Emmy turned to face him. He was looking at her curiously, his beautiful eyes deep and warm, and she couldn't resist falling into the fantasy.

'You remind me of someone I met once,' she teased him playfully.

His eyebrows arched. 'Who was that?'

'Oh, he was a pirate.'

'A *pirate*?' His grin flashed in the moonlight.

'He came to the islands looking for treasure. His name was Ramon and he was a rogue and I couldn't resist him. He was playful and fun and impossible to say no to.'

'Was he?' A tantalising thread in his voice drew her nearer. 'Well, you remind me of someone I met once, too,' he said. 'She wasn't like any other woman I'd met before.'

'No?'

'She emerged from the water in this stunning bikini, a voluptuous nymph.'

'That's what caught your eye, huh?' She giggled. 'Always the bikini.'

'What can I say?' He laughed. 'It emphasised her spectacular curves and flaming-red hair. But it was her artless confidence that stopped me in my tracks. She looked so liberated in her wild environment—open and innocent and it turned out she *was* a rare creature in disguise. She was a bona fide fire-breathing dragon and she let me into her secret world.'

'A dragon?'

'The best kind. Beautiful, every inch was a different sort of treasure.'

'Ramon showed me a secret world of his own too,' she whispered huskily. 'Dance with me.'

His gaze flared. 'Dance? There's no music.'

'You know we make our own.' She didn't just dance with him, she danced for him. Teasing her way out of the silk dress.

'You're so damn sexy,' he muttered hoarsely. 'I just want to…'

'To what?' she teased. Because she knew very well and she wanted it every bit as much.

And suddenly this was *her* night. Nothing—

no reticence or fear—held her back. It was like that night on the beach when a pirate had appeared and breathed the fierceness within her to life. Only now it was better. Now she understood more what there was to be had with him. And now she understood just what it was she was feeling and how deep it ran and there was no way she could not express it. Not now he was before her again, gazing intently, his jaw slack, his breathing roughened as she danced closer still.

'Emmy...'

It was a cross between a warning and a plea and it only made her burn hotter and her smile more sultry and her heart more loving. And she wanted to love him so very much. She wanted not to hide, not to have to be afraid, not to have to stay silent as she had in other ways for so long.

The truth that had hit her earlier tonight was so huge, there was no hiding it, no denying it and, in this moonlit madness, she didn't even want to try. Instead she let it release—streaming from every pore. Every sweep of her hands, every suck of her mouth, every arch of her hips, spelled out her passion for him. She couldn't stop her own response, her own desire and discovering again the joy of his powerful, guttural response. The need to prove in this one, most basic and instinctive of ways consumed her—that she was utterly his.

CHAPTER ELEVEN

JAVIER STEALTHILY MOVED across the bedroom floor, not wishing to wake her this early. The sun wasn't even a glimmer on the water yet, but his mind was riffing on too many things for him to sleep. Too many uncomfortable things. And suddenly he couldn't stay here... he couldn't float endlessly in the middle of the Pacific Ocean, eating and swimming and sleeping...

Last night had been...*successful*? He should, in theory, be delighted at the way the hotel re-furbishment was going and the welcome he'd received from local business leaders. He ought to be delighted at how popular Emmy's photo had been in that line-up celebrating the re-gion—and how touched she'd been he'd used it. And frankly, he ought to be in the recovery position and having extra oxygen tubed in, given how explosively passionate they'd been together last night—how devastating her sexy ministrations on deck had been. She had been pure feminine strength, pure fire and he shook just thinking about it.

So in theory, he ought not to be able to move right now at all.

Instead, the *only* thing he wanted to do was move. The discomfort that had begun as a mere irritating itch beneath his skin had inflamed into a sharp ache that rendered him unable to remain still. He went into the onboard office and focused on a multitude of meaningless tasks. The emails that could wait for replies, he tapped out lengthy responses to at three in the morning. He dictated longer missives for his assistant back in the States to act on later. He listed more things to be done by the rest of his team, brainstormed next developments and new ideas. He checked the global share-price indices, repeatedly, and scanned headlines of online papers and journals. It was all very deliberate and focused—as if by keeping busy again, he could ignore that problematic feeling increasing inside. But though he tried and tried, he couldn't avoid the raging possessiveness emerging within him.

It wasn't a nice feeling. Worse was that it wasn't within his control.

It wasn't regarding Luke—he was different, somehow. There was possessiveness, protectiveness, certainly. But it was embedded within a rock-solid certainty. Javier knew, no matter what, that he would always be there for his son. *That* was a surety.

But the look on Emmy's face last night when she'd risen over his body. The light in her eyes? The tenderness in her touch? That had been too much. Far too much.

And that sense of elusiveness that he couldn't cope with? It was destroying him now.

Instead of being able to breathe easy and just enjoy this passing phase with her, he found himself flexing his fist as if he could hold onto the invisible. Or the impossible. But instead of grasping and getting only air, he knew he needed to push right away. Now.

Because he didn't just like her touch, he ached for her *attention*. And attention, he knew, eventually wandered. It ought not to matter—he assured himself it *didn't* matter. It was just that it hadn't been long enough to burn their chemistry yet. She'd teased him, questioning about how that would fade, but while he'd laughed, he'd been sure it would. It always had before. Perhaps the problem was because he was out of his usual sphere. It was time to return to the real world—not the isolated oasis of unique, protected creatures. The sooner the better.

'I need to go back to New York.' He couldn't even look into her eyes; he didn't want those blues to magnify the nugget of regret lodging in his chest. 'I have work commitments. Some meetings I can't miss.'

'When?' Wariness muted her voice.

'As soon as we're packed.'

'You wouldn't let Luke and I stay here and come back when you're done?'

His gut tightened in instant rebellion at the thought, not just of leaving Luke, but of leaving her. That she'd even asked aggravated the irritation that had been festering for days.

'I'm sorry, that was a stupid thing to ask.' She spoke again swiftly before he had the chance to reply. 'That was just me being...'

Cautious. And Javier could understand it on a rational level. This was her home and Luke's birthplace. But his gut roiled with perceived rejection. *Nowhere* was going to be as good as here for her.

'We'll come back often.' He coughed the rasp from his throat. 'I'll need to for work anyway.'

As always, once Javier set a plan in motion, it was enacted swiftly and precisely. Emmy counted as she breathed, trying to stay calm and not fall to pieces as she left the superyacht that had become 'home' in a shockingly short time period. They used the helicopter again from the boat back to Santa Cruz, where she insisted on seeing Connie to say goodbye and reassure her she'd bring Luke back again soon. Then they'd hopped to Quito and begun the journey to New York. The first-class cabin was luxurious but she couldn't relax. Not even having Thomas to entertain Luke helped, it just gave her more time to ruminate on what was going to happen once they got to Javier's home. And apart from that one query, Javier hadn't bothered her. Hadn't chatted with her. Hadn't shared a laugh with her. It was as if he'd left already—lost in staring at his laptop screen, a frown of concentration and contemplation.

There was no hint—no look, no touch, no

murmur—of the magic they'd shared last night. No sign that he'd noticed how much of herself she'd given him then—because, truth be told, she'd given him everything last night. With her arms, her hands, her mouth…her *heart*.

And how could he not have felt that? How could he not know?

Yet it seemed he didn't. Or worse, if he did, he wanted to pretend as if it hadn't happened. Because he was silent and he didn't see her. All he seemed to want was to escape. The problem was they were each to become a permanent pillar in the other's life.

But not in the way she wanted.

So what happened when this 'chemistry' he felt for her finally faded? Where did that leave her? Because it wasn't ever going to fade for her. It was built from something more solid than pheromones now and she knew her heart was about to be broken. Yet because of Luke, she was bound to Javier for the rest of her life. She'd be there, watching like a glued-to-the-pavement passer-by when he found new lovers. And there'd be plenty of them. And when he eventually found a woman he wanted to make his *wife*… She was sure that would happen, despite his declarations to the contrary. He was a fantastic father and an incredible lover and a generous, *all in* kind of person. So when he finally truly fell for someone, he wouldn't hesitate. And he'd never do to Luke what had been done to him. He'd ensure his firstborn child was always kept close, in the very heart of his new family's embrace. While Emerald would be glued in place—on the outside looking in.

'Emmy?'

'Mmm?'

He was frowning at her from across the aisle of the plane. 'What are you thinking about?'

'Nothing.'

'You look like you're about to cry.'

She felt like it. Instead she dragged on a smile. 'I was just drifting…miles away. Sorry.'

'No need to be sorry.' But he looked sombre. 'I promise you'll come back to the islands often.'

It wasn't leaving the islands hurting her heart. Even if they were to stay, the outlook would remain the same. A lonely, heartbroken future.

Javier's residential building in Manhattan was near the financial district. As sophisticated and gleamingly stylish as she'd have expected. Totally the showstopper piece required for a financial *wunderkind* turned property billion-aire.

'A room has been partially kitted out as Luke's nursery,' he said as he carried their son in his arms and led her through the spacious apartment. 'But you can do more with it if you'd like.'

She glanced around the timelessly styled suite. Two large frames hung with perfect symmetry on the wall opposite Luke's bed—one held the very first photo of Luke with her, moments after his birth. The other was the photo she'd taken of Javier with Luke swimming off the coast. There was not, she noted with a dull hit to her heart, a photo of the three of them *together*.

'Thomas has the guest wing,' Javier added. 'And he'll use the apartment I have for my staff on the level two below this during his weekends.'

She rather envied the separate small living room, kitchenette, bedroom and bathroom that was for Thomas's exclusive use.

'There's a computer on the desk for you, also

a security card, access code, numbers for a driver if you need one. All the information is in the folder beside it.'

'Thank you.' She glanced and saw the boxes of brand-new things—laptop, phone, watch.

Emotionally fraught, she saw her bags had been put straight into the master suite. Javier's large bed dominated the room and she quickly turned away from it, almost bumping into him behind her.

'I have to go to the office.' Javier stepped back brusquely. 'I'll be a few hours.'

'Of course.'

Yes, his walls were up again and his mind was clearly elsewhere—as it had been the whole trip. It seemed he couldn't wait to get away from them both and she was so hurt. Had he seen what she'd felt last night? Was this why he was rejecting her now? And her anger began to grow—why couldn't he at least talk to her about it? Why not be honest?

She gave Thomas the rest of the day off to organise his things. Finally alone with Luke, she explored the large apartment. It taught her nothing new about Javier—there were no family pictures anywhere other than those two in

Luke's room. But given what he'd told her, she wasn't surprised at that. The bookcases were filled with non-fiction on a variety of eclectic subjects. The art hanging in the living area and the sculptures on plinths in the vestibule were probably investments. As was the entire building, of course. It wasn't a home that revealed anything about the inner life or personality of its owner. It was simply pristine and utterly comfortable—as restful and perfect as the hotels he was becoming famous for.

In the gleaming kitchen, the fridge was already filled with organic, nutritious baby food provided by a boutique service Thomas had tracked down. Though, now they were ensconced in their new home, he would prepare most of Luke's meals from scratch. Javier had told her he liked to order food in from any of the numerous restaurants nearby.

So, it seemed she wasn't needed for any kind of housekeeping or cooking support… or anything much else.

Emmy took Luke for a walk around the neighbourhood to familiarise herself with the area. Then, while her son napped, she swallowed her pride and set up the new laptop

Javier had had delivered. She would search online for possible work. Truthfully Javier's thoughts had been helpful and she loved the idea of doing something with her photography. She had several skills and she'd figure something out; she always had in the past. But she got side-tracked looking at an online article about Javier. It referenced his staff—personal assistants, lawyers, accountants. He oversaw a whole empire she knew little about. Yet he'd talked to her about his plans earlier in the week on the boat when they'd both been distracting themselves from their own lust. He'd taken the time to answer her questions about what he did and why. He'd asked for her own experiences and advice on how to continue the legacy of the Flores Foundation. They'd debated the need and meaning of the voluntary programmes, the importance of sustainability. And she'd enjoyed every moment of those discussions.

She refocused and searched online for possible jobs, brainstorming ideas on paper as she went. Hours passed and she fed and bathed Luke, reading to him. Then dined herself.

Javier still didn't return.

She curled up in one of the large cosy armchairs in the library and chose a movie to watch. She was behind on all the latest releases and Javier had subscriptions to all the streaming services.

'Emmy?'

She stirred. The room was in darkness; the sound on the television had been lowered. She must've fallen asleep in front of the movie. Javier was standing a short distance away. Wearing only boxers and a tee, he'd apparently just showered. She sat up, embarrassed that he'd caught her. But at the same time, her mouth dried. He was so gorgeous.

'Have you eaten?' he asked.

'Thanks, yes.' She unfolded her legs and ran her hands down her thighs. 'I got a delivery from the Italian on that list you left. It was delicious.'

'Good.' His reply seemed distant. 'Look—' he ran his hand through his hair, his expression grim '—I know we've only been back one day, but I have to take an overnight trip to Miami tomorrow. I thought we'd all go.'

Emmy stilled. His work schedule was going to be challenging for her to find something of her own. Did he really want her to go too? 'If that's what you want.'

Silence stretched. In the semi-darkness she couldn't read his eyes.

'I'm sorry I was home later than I'd wanted to be.' He rubbed his arm and took a step closer to her. 'I've checked on Luke. He's fast asleep.' His lips suddenly curved, softening the seriousness in his stance. 'You were too. But you need to be somewhere more comfortable.'

She didn't reply as he took her hands in his and tugged her to her feet. He didn't say anything more as he led her to his bedroom and that huge bed. He'd turned the covers down already. She sank into the soft linen, too tired to resist her own desires. She wanted the pleasure he gave her. She couldn't deny herself, despite that growing warning within. And in seconds that alarm was silenced anyway—drowned in the physical delight washing through her. And Javier's mouth and hands were as hungry and as desperate as her own. It was as if they were both determined to keep too busy and keep mouths too full to let secrets slip.

CHAPTER TWELVE

'THOMAS HAS LUKE,' Javier muttered when she stirred as he left the bed early the next morning. 'Sleep in while you can. I'll be back this afternoon to take us to the airport.'

Sleeping in was an impossibility but Emmy didn't reply. When he'd gone she rolled onto her back and stared at the ceiling, hardening her resolve. They'd spent the night attempting to satiate that physical desire with a lengthy, wordless expression of pure lust. But the playful, passionate element of that night at the gala had gotten lost somewhere along the way. Last night had felt more desperate, more frantic— to her at least. And she *had* been desperate to hold back how she really felt. Her heart ached, but she knew she couldn't hold back the truth in those moments of intimacy again. She *would* end up telling him how she felt.

And that would be terrible. That would be an exposure worse than any. Worse than the fear of people finding out and judging her for her family's actions. She would be so vulnerable. Because she knew—absolutely—that what she felt for Javier was not reciprocated by him.

He'd told her, quite openly, right from the start—even that first night on the beach—he didn't want a long-term lover. He didn't want a wife. He didn't want a real relationship with her. He believed, not in love, but in chemistry. And in his world, that chemistry would all be used up soon enough.

But he'd not really told her why. He'd mentioned his father, his mother's remarriage. But he'd not talked to her about how that had all really felt. He'd been almost glib and joked it off before changing the subject as quickly as possible. He'd not wanted to open up to her.

And wasn't that fair enough?

Except she'd opened up to him. She'd told him of her shame of her family, of her own mistakes, of her own choices. And he'd accepted her.

But he wouldn't allow her to do the same for him. He didn't want to the same way she did.

So she now had to accept that.

Suddenly this Miami trip was a saviour.

It was her opportunity to take the time she needed to clear her head and make the move she needed to make. She knew Javier could offer Luke everything and he'd begun to love Luke as much as anyone could. He'd become a wonderful father who wanted to be there for his son.

Emmy couldn't ask anything more of him than that. He didn't have to love *her* too.

Her problem was *she* was in love with him. It had snuck up on her so quickly and it was so much more than that wickedly wonderful passion they shared. He was gorgeous—strong and fit. But he was also funny and loyal and intelligent and special. But it was her problem and hers alone. She couldn't let it negatively impact on Luke. Or on Javier.

But she needed time to process and move past her disappointment and heartbreak. She could work out a plan that she could live with long term given the time and space to do that. Because she couldn't continue this as it currently was. She couldn't live this close with him not actually wanting her in the same way. She couldn't keep giving of herself, couldn't fall deeper and deeper still with every kiss, with every conversation...

And she needed to face the reality of her future with Javier as a loving, active parent in Luke's life. She needed to let Javier take him, to face time apart from them both and get used to being on her own for periods of time. Because even if she and Javier were really together as a couple, that would happen at times. They wouldn't all be able to travel together always. So she needed to start now and deal with it. And she could do that. For Luke. For Javier. And for herself.

Fortunately Javier Torres wasn't the only one who could make swift plans. Emmy too knew how to get things done. She had years of survival behind her. She could handle this.

'Can you take Luke down to the car, please, Thomas?' Emmy asked the nanny when Javier arrived in the early afternoon as he'd said he would. 'Javier and I just need a moment first.'

She saw the questioning look Javier shot her, but he said nothing while Thomas and Luke were still present. Emmy kissed her son's head and indulged in a tiny extra-tight squeeze before handing her most precious bundle to the hyper-efficient, affable nanny.

'What's up?' Javier asked once the elevator door had slid shut.

Emmy locked her knees to try to combat the stupidly nervous tremble within. 'I'm not coming with you.'

Javier cocked his head, his gaze sharpening. 'You what?'

'I'm not coming with you to Miami.' She cleared her throat and spoke more forcefully. 'I don't want to.'

'And you decide to announce this now, when we're all packed and Thomas and Luke are already in the car?'

'It makes no difference to you whether I come or not.'

'On the contrary, it makes a very great difference to me.' He actually smiled at her.

Seriously? Was he reducing this moment to *sex*? Another distraction in the form of a joke? She stared back at him sombrely; well, that would be right—that was all this was to him.

His smile faded. 'Emmy—'

'I'm not going,' she said in a low voice. 'You

go. Take Luke.' She blinked back the appalling storm of hot tears that threatened to spill.

For a split second his jaw slackened. 'Why? What's wrong?' He lifted his head sharply. 'What are you going to do while we're gone? Will you be here when we get back?'

With one doubting question he sliced away the last stable ground from beneath her feet.

'Did you really need to ask that?' She stared at him, hurt. 'And you say *I* expect the worst from people?' She crossed her arms in front of her chest, holding herself tightly. 'You do too, Javier. You expect it from me. You don't trust me. I don't think you ever have.'

'That's not what I meant.' He jerked his arm to the side and drew in a deep breath. 'Is it because you're tired?' he asked in a determinedly reasonable tone. 'Because I can reschedule. I'll fly early in the morning and back late tomorrow night. Then neither of you need accompany me.'

His offer of an alternative hurt her even more. Because he was *trying*, he wanted to do what was 'right'. But that wasn't enough for *her* needs. Because he was still holding his own truths out on her.

'That's unsustainable in the long run.' She shook her head firmly. 'The travel you need to do is hard enough—you need to be at your best for your business. And for Luke. You need to take him and stay overnight tonight. Come back when you're done.'

He stood very still. 'In the long run?'

'We need to start as we're going to carry on. This is one night. I know you'll care for him,' she said.

He watched her with an intent frown as if trying to parse some other meaning to her words.

'Look, you're taking Thomas.' She tried to lighten her tone so she didn't sound as if this were some death knell. Even though it felt like it. 'You know, the nanny with all the amazing qualifications. And he'll be with you, his father. Who loves him.'

'You're happy to let Luke go, just like that?'

She pressed her lips together for a moment to bite back the pain. 'One night away is nothing compared to what you've already missed out on. And I'm not asking you to miss out on another night with him now I know how much it matters to you. I wouldn't do that to

you. Go.' She was angry with him for not moving already—for making this harder than she
wanted it to be. 'I know you'll care for him. I
know you'll bring him back safe and well and
happy.'

'So you're doing this for my benefit?' he que-
ried quietly. 'But what is it that *you're* going
to do?'

She didn't want to discuss her plans with
him; she wasn't ready to yet. 'I just need some
time.' She still tried to play it lightly.

'Not away from Luke,' he said with annoying
perceptiveness. 'You're nearly in tears at the
thought of being apart from him for one night.'

She stiffened, trying to stem the emotion
from leaking out of every pore.

'So, no need to offer any more clues.' He
stepped right in front of her. 'It's *me* you need
some time from.'

His insistence broke her.

'Yes,' she gritted. 'It's you.'

He stiffened but he didn't step back. 'Why?'
He folded his arms and stared right into her
eyes. 'What have I done?'

She shook her head at his continued push.
'Don't be cruel.'

'Cruel?' Shock—and accusation—crackled in his voice. 'All I'm asking for is honesty. I want to understand, Emmy. Have I done something wrong? It shouldn't be that difficult to tell me.'

The face that he had no idea how difficult it was for her to even face him right now was so very telling. He had no idea of how she really felt. Of how he was hurting her. She glanced away from him.

'I can't do this—' she muttered.

'Be honest?'

'That is so very you, Javier.' She inhaled sharply. 'You seek *answers*. But not intimacy.'

'What does that even mean?'

'You want to know things, so that way you can provide a neat solution and keep everything in your control. So you can pat yourself on the back, satisfied you've ticked all the boxes and done all you could. But you never make *yourself* vulnerable. You never offer all the answers of your own.' She broke off. She didn't want to slam him. She didn't want to debate this when she was still figuring it out for herself. 'Look, by inviting me to travel, you're trying to include me in everything with Luke, I get that. And I appreciate it, especially when I wasn't as fair at the start. But I'm just an added extra you don't really want or need. And I don't want to be that extra burden on you. Right now the financial aspect is too much already. I'm trying to work on that.'

'You don't need to—'

'I do. For my own dignity I need independence.'

'I have enough resources to support—'

'Don't you understand? That's *not* what I want from you.'

'Then what is?'

She stared at him. 'You don't want me to say what I really want. You won't want to give it to me.'

'Why not tell me and let me decide? Instead you're throwing a grenade out the door with me and not being brave enough to deal with the fallout. I'm trying to do what's right for *all* of us. Most especially for Luke.'

'As am I,' she tossed back hotly, her handle on her emotions slipping further still.

'Really? *You're* the one who won't stick around anywhere long enough to establish real relationships. Who ran away to one of the world's most remote places where other people pretty much only passed through. And you only stayed there because having Luke anchored you. You're terrified to trust anyone. The second you think you're at risk, you run— only this time you can't, you're stuck, so you're pushing back on me. Why not be brave enough to be honest about what the damn problem is? Why not fight for yourself, Emmy?'

'What do you think I've just done?' She glared at him. 'I've just told you…' She trailed off in shock as everything rippled upwards from the depths in which she'd long suppressed it and she could no longer hold a word of it back. 'I've been afraid for so long. Afraid of my family. Afraid of losing my place. Afraid people would find out about everything and they'd then reject me—because they have before. I lived on a knife edge all the time, just waiting for everything to go wrong, and that was a horrible way to live—'

'How many times do I have to tell you I don't care that half your family are criminals? It doesn't bother—'

'I know you don't care, Javier,' she snapped

harshly. 'I know that. *That's* the point. *That's* the problem here.'

He froze, his eyes wide and his face whitening.

'You know what?' she questioned, losing her control entirely. 'You were right—I did seal myself away in a safe sanctuary. I'd not realised the extent to which I'd hidden away on the edge of the world, avoiding mostly everyone so I didn't have to fear that judgement. But while it was paradise, I was missing so much. Then I met you and I had Luke and opened my world right up. Because I can't deny him what I denied myself. I can't keep him hidden away in some sanctuary where he doesn't get everything he deserves. You were so right about that. But *I* deserve more too.' She shook inside as every emotion, every yearning poured forth. 'You want me to carve open my wounds and expose my bleeding heart, Javier? Fine. I'll do that. Here's my honesty. I can't continue with the uncertainty of you "fading" on me, while I *know* the feelings I have for you won't. Because I don't just feel lust, Javier. I've fallen in love with you. But you don't want to love me.'

He stared at her, an arrested—and appalled—expression in his eyes.

'I know you believe you don't want marriage or a long-term relationship—because it always ends in divorce, right?' she barrelled along despite that horror in his face. 'You tell yourself *nothing* lasts. Which means you don't have to make the *effort*. It lets you off the hook. You don't have to try. *Why bother? It won't last anyway.* It's lazy, Javier. And it's cowardly.' She glared at him. 'Yet here you are, determinedly building beautiful buildings to last longer than your own lifetime. And even though you know there might be some seismic shift in the earth that breaks it apart anyway—you still go ahead and build it. But in your personal life, you can't accept that some things might be beyond all your control but it's worth braving it anyway. That it's worth the risk…but you won't open yourself to the threat of that chaos. *I'm* not worth that risk to you. You're happy to sleep with me. You're happy to foot all my bills… but you're not happy to truly commit to me, because this is just "chemistry", right?' Hurt ignited rage and every emotion poured from her in a torrent of sadness and regret. 'But it isn't—not for me. And I can't live with that uncertainty and insecurity.'

Concern tightened his features and that expressionless—*dead*—look in his eyes that she'd grown to *loathe* emerged.

'And you keep holding out on me,' she cried bitterly when he didn't respond. 'You won't open up to me. You use sex, or a laugh or your work or just this…just silence. You won't ever say what you're really, actually *feeling*.'

'Emmy…'

It was the pity in his voice that did her in and destroyed the last of her hope. 'No, don't—' She held up a hand, warding him off. Warning him not to step nearer. 'Don't try to tell me that it's not just me, that it's any woman. Any one. Because here's the thing. I know you're capable of love. I've seen it—you love Luke. But that's different. That's snuck up on you in a primal way that you have no choice over. You can't deny it. And that *is* love. It is too big for someone to contain it, or conceal it…it leaks out. Like it's leaking out of me right now. But you can deny it for me, because you don't love *me*. So I can't let things go on as they are knowing you can't give me what I want. You don't feel the same. And I get it. I'm not…what you really want. Fine. But you don't get to monopolise the best of me. Not all of my time in this part of my life. I deserve more. I've missed out on so much and I can't let myself settle for not good enough again. So I can't… I can't stay in this…undefined…sleeping-together arrangement. It's tearing me apart. It's destroying everything I've built for myself.'

'You're saying I'm destroying you?'

'My sleeping with you is. My living with you like a lover is.' She made herself lift her voice and finish this. 'I know we need to deal with each other. And I'm sorry because I'm not in a position to be fully independent from you yet—not in Manhattan. Not where you need Luke to be. So you and I both have to compromise. I hate it, but I have to accept your offer of living space, only for as long as it takes to set myself up independently. But I won't travel with you. I want you to take Luke. I don't want you to miss out on any more time with him.'

'Wow, that's so generous of you.' His eyes flashed like shining black stones. 'You're afraid of judgement, but you're not afraid to dish it out as far as I'm concerned. I made one mistake when I didn't tell you my full name, and you've never wanted to forgive me—'

'No. It isn't about that. I'm long over that. It's not about forgiving, but what you can't— won't—give me. You offer everything material, but nothing precious. Yes, I might have hidden away in some ways on the islands, but *you're* the one keeping safe. You're the one refusing to open up emotionally. You won't tell me so much more than your name…you can't even tell me properly *why* you even needed to do that. Why did you want a break from being you, Javier? Why didn't you like your own company that night?' She flung her head back as he stood there, pale and silent. 'We're different people, with different needs. And we had this wonderful night together, but that was supposed to be it. With Luke, we've been brought back together and we succumbed to that attraction again. But ultimately we want different things. And that's okay. I just need some space to work through how this is going to be.'

'So when I get back?'

'I won't be in your bed waiting for you. I'm not sleeping with you any more. We're co-parents. And that's it.'

'You think it can just end between us—just like that? Emmy.' He shook his head in rampant disbelief. 'Last night we—'

'It's *over*,' she snapped fiercely. 'That part has to be over. Please don't try to change my mind. Please respect my choice. Please don't make a joke of what I'm trying to tell you. Or I *will* have to leave.'

He stared at her.

'We both want what's best for Luke, but I also need to do what's best for *me* in this. And that is not to be with you.' She gazed at him, so hurt but still unable to let go of the last remnants of hope. 'And the worst thing is the fact that I'm *always* going to want more from you. I'm going to want more than you can *ever* give me,' she said. 'I don't want the *things*. I don't want the fancy boat or amazing bling or designer dresses. But *you* can only give me the things.' She looked up at him. 'You can't give me the love and trust and intimacy I want from you. It's not there.'

He said nothing. He didn't argue with her. Didn't deny the truth. Didn't tell her any of the words her foolish heart ached to hear.

'I didn't want to *say* any of this,' she groaned

248 SECRETS MADE IN PARADISE

sadly. 'Why did you push? Why couldn't you just leave me? Why did you have to be so mean?' She hated that she'd lost control and revealed everything of herself. It was humiliating. But worse, it was painful because it only proved what she'd already known. He didn't love her. He didn't want her the way she wanted him. 'This is why I need time away from *you.*' She was furious with him and herself. 'Please go now. I promise I'll be here when you get back. I would never leave my son.'

'But you'd leave me.'

'Yes.' A million times *yes.* She could barely see him through the tearful haze in her eyes. Right now she wanted to run away from him faster than she'd ever run from anything in her life.

CHAPTER THIRTEEN

JAVIER STALKED OUT of the building, his stomach tight.

'Let's go.' He jerked his head at his driver and chose to sit in the front passenger seat and not engage with his son, safely tucked in the back with the nanny. He needed to cool down and process before he could speak to anyone. Right now he was raging inside.

Emmy's rejection of their physical relationship was a rejection of *him*. Her refusal to travel with him on this, the shortest of trips, was a rejection of *him*. If she had complete freedom of choice—no small son to think of—then she would utterly reject him. She would walk out and not look back and never return. He knew it. He'd seen it before.

Her words? Her passion? Telling him she was in love with him in one breath and asking him to avoid her altogether in the next? She didn't want him. She didn't love him. If she did, why would she instantly do the one thing that would hurt him the most? Why would she shut him out?

So he didn't believe her declaration. Not for a second. She had been isolated for too long. She'd been lonely. She'd been inexperienced. She'd hit some sort of high from the companionship and closeness that she'd never really had before and confused that with…what she thought was love. In fact, he raged inwardly, it wasn't actually *him* she thought she was in love with. It was the change in circumstances. It was—he hated to realise—a kind of gratitude, or, worse, some sort of sick Stockholm syndrome, because they were bound to each other because of their baby. Trapped together, so her hormones were helping her make the best of it by believing her to be…in love with him, the father of her child.

He flew to Miami. On the flight he calmed down enough to read to Luke, the same little story over and over, softly murmuring the rhyme for the entire journey. Anything to avoid the thoughts—the echo of her words—circling over and over in his head instead.

But then his little son slept and he decided

to work late in the hotel, only it was impossible to concentrate. So, late at night, he abandoned the effort and tried to sleep. But then, in his dreams he was transfixed by the vision of Emerald Jones, fire-breathing beauty—promising everything in one instant and stealing it back the next.

And her words kept echoing. Her accusations. Her truths.

Because what she'd said was right, was it not? He didn't want a relationship. And maybe they'd been overcomplicating things by continuing to sleep together even though they'd left the islands. Maybe this was the right time to end that side of things. It was only sex, after all. And getting clarification, boundaries, back would be good. That was what he'd wanted all along, wasn't it? But more phrases she'd thrown at him kept echoing in his mind.

You don't get to monopolise the best of me. Not all of my time...

Did that mean she wanted to be free to meet someone else? Rationally he knew that she should. Of course. And she *would*. She was a stunningly vibrant woman who ought to be scooped up by some guy and adored for all eternity.

He flinched and had to shift position in his suddenly uncomfortable bed. He couldn't stand the idea of some other jerk adoring her. He winced at his dog-in-the-manger attitude. He didn't want her but didn't want anyone else to have her either?

Things—okay, yes, relationships—*didn't* last. He'd seen it time and time again. He'd borne the brunt of the fallout. And it was his own fault for reigniting that passion with her. Except there was no way he could have resisted at the time. And nor had she been able to. He'd been right about that 'chemistry' at least. It was uncontainable.

But he also knew that now she'd made her decision, she would stick to it. Emmy had determination and strength and this choice of hers would last. *She* was one person who could remain constant and true.

And that sudden realisation? That made his whole chest ache all over again.

He doggedly forced focus in the meetings the next day. He refused to let his staff down or his business slide because of his personal life. But he concluded the schedule as quickly as he could, returning to Luke. To hold and quietly vow to his son that he would never, ever leave him. Because being left—being rejected—*sucked*. And it hurt. And it *damaged*.

And it had happened to Javier before. More than once.

Only he'd never really told her that, had he? And he'd certainly never really stopped to consider just how it had damaged *him*.

He paused, making himself reflect on those moments in his past that he'd chosen to forget for so long. Those most painful ones—what kinds of warped lessons had they taught him?

Was what she'd said fair? Had he held back from her?

He couldn't sit still to consider the answer; he knew it already. But at the time she'd said it, he'd been too busy being hurt—too busy feeling that horror of rejection again—to be able to think clearly enough to respond.

Only now he had the time to think. And it wasn't pleasant.

Was he going to let the scars from the past stop him from seeing the future that might be possible? The chance that was right in front of him?

On the flight back to New York Luke slept again and Javier closed his eyes too—trying to figure out what to say to her when he saw her next. But he didn't see her. She'd moved her few clothes from his room to that last spare bedroom on the far side of Luke's. So Javier did the decent thing and went to work again late at night—giving her time to reunite with their baby without him watching.

An hour later he stared at the list she'd messaged through, barely biting back the urge to sprint back to the apartment and storm into her new room and tell her exactly what he thought of her 'timetable'—an appalling co-parenting arrangement in which they completely avoided each other. He pushed away that instinctive wound—his own petulant assumption that it was a rejection of him. That *he* wasn't enough. He was overreacting. But she'd struck a nerve. And how was it her hit could hurt this hard?

He got home late and the apartment was too quiet. He stole into Luke's room and watched him sleep a while. Inexorably his attention was drawn to the photo he'd ordered hung on

Luke's nursery wall. The portrait of Emmy and Luke, moments after Luke's arrival, had struck him the second he'd seen it. All the emotions rose every time he looked at it—protectiveness, possessiveness. They overwhelmed him. He lifted the picture from Luke's wall and put it in his own room. He went to sleep looking at them and they were the first things he saw when he woke. But the misery rose, the rage blurred and slowly the truth settled. He needed that picture—it was his own aide-memoire—because they were the two most precious things in his life.

But now he knew the picture alone wasn't enough. He wanted the real things—*both* of them with him, all of the time. And it was only now that she'd pushed him away that he realised that he, too, struggled with secrets, and struggled without certainty. He'd thought he had it all sorted—had offered her 'everything' he could in a half-assed, cowardly way. He'd suggested she stay with him, offering her no security. He was a jerk. But he'd not realised it himself—not until now. So his ineptitude, his silence of the other day when she'd opened up and hurled all her thoughts and feelings at his head, appealing to his heart…that had hurt her. It had hurt him too. Because he'd kept his heart buried away for so very long he'd just about forgotten it was there.

He'd *never* had emotional security. But he wanted his son to have it—to give it to him. He wanted to do that for Emmy too—so very differently and so very much. And she, more than anyone except perhaps himself, needed that certainty. She needed to hear the truth. She needed absolute honesty before she would believe. And he needed her to forgive him and to believe in him. This separation—he realised far too late—was the antithesis of what he wanted. He wanted *everything* with her.

He'd been so self-defensive, so focused on building his walls, he'd become blind to his own emotions. All the things he'd done—not just providing for her, but listening to her, laughing with her, wanting to bring her out, making love to her—they'd all been the actions of a man falling deeply in love.

He just hadn't seen it in himself. And she'd not seen it either and that was on him. Because he'd been so damn defensive he'd hidden it too well from her. She'd opened up to him—she'd been so brave, so vulnerable, so trusting in him. But he'd *hurt* her.

So while he'd long been decisive, he knew whatever action he took now, whatever gesture he tried to think of, it wasn't going to be enough. Because it was the *words* that were required. Words—or lack of—could hurt, but words could also heal. Sometimes stupid words could be forgiven. And honest words would be believed. He hoped so, anyway. He had to think that it might be possible in this case.

Because Emerald Jones, he finally realised, was his gorgeous dragon—she'd made him believe in something he'd thought was mere myth or fairy tale. But it was magic and real—it was hot and wonderful and scary as hell. She'd made him believe in the existence of love.

CHAPTER FOURTEEN

'THOMAS?' EMMY WALKED into the apartment. 'Luke?'

She listened but heard no reply. It was four days since her blow-up with Javier. He'd taken Luke and gone for the night. She'd indulged in a horrendous crying jag. Then she'd wiped a cold flannel over her face and moved her stuff into the spare bedroom farthest from Javier's. She'd spent the night alternately wiping her eyes with that cold flannel and giving herself a pep talk and desperately trying to find a distraction for herself. Find work. Study. Survive.

She'd managed to avoid him mostly since their return. He'd been gracious enough to stay away for her reunion with Luke.

He'd apparently agreed to her suggestion of him leaving for work later, so he had time with Luke in the mornings. She lay on her bed and pretended to read or sleep or do something—

anything—until she heard the front door close and was certain he'd left for the day.

She had dinner early, with Luke, and retreated to her room again when Javier returned home for the night. She'd booked onto an online course to improve her photography skills and researched some courses on management for charitable entities. She had a strong idea of what she wanted.

Thomas was the epitome of discretion and kindly courteous, leaving her with Luke as she needed the time to hold her baby and express love to him. But right now her baby wasn't here. There was nothing to distract her again from the heartache and hopelessness of loving Javier or the anger within that she'd missed out.

Why couldn't she have more? Why couldn't she have it all?

She walked towards the lounge, absorbing the emptiness of the apartment like a hit to the side of the head. But an achingly familiar, tall figure turned at the window. Her heart leapt into her throat. Not from fear, but worse—joy. The bubble of rapture burst a split second later as she remembered.

'Javier.' She stopped on the threshold. 'I'm sorry. I didn't realise you were home early.'

He looked cold and tired. His powerful form was half hidden by a loose black turtleneck and jeans. He hadn't shaved, and his hair stood in tufts as if he'd been tugging on it or had just not bothered with it for the day because he had other things on his mind.

'Don't apologise.' He watched her steadily but didn't step closer. 'Thomas's taken Luke to the park for an hour or so. I cancelled my meetings.'

Warily she waited in the doorway. It was obvious he had something to say and she could hardly walk away before he'd had the chance. But it was too soon for her—that aching wish inside her threatened to leak out all over again.

'We can't go on like this, Emmy. We can't keep avoiding each other.'

Her heart pounded. 'Actually, I think it's working well,' she argued stiffly, striving to retain self-control. Seeing him as little as possible was absolutely for the best. Because just seeing him like this, now, made parts of her ache in ways she wanted to avoid for ever.

His jaw tightened and his teeth clamped. 'I'm

not well and I don't believe for a second you are either.'

She flinched.

'I was a jerk to you.' His voice was low and didn't sound like him at all.

She shook her head. She didn't want him to apologise, to be nice to her. She didn't want any sort of sympathy or pretence of caring because they'd happened to create a child together. She wanted to forget what she'd said, forget their physical intimacy and just move forward with new distance between them. It was the *only* way she could survive it.

'I shouldn't have said what I said,' she said hurriedly. 'It wasn't fair. Please forget it. We've just…we need to move on.'

'I'm never going to forget what you said, Emmy. Not ever.' He stepped closer but stopped as he saw her reaction to his words. 'And I don't want to move on.'

Emmy put her hand on the doorjamb for support. Caught in that doorway, she couldn't step either forward or back. It was as if she were trapped in a kind of purgatory.

'You told me you're in love with me,' he said quietly.

Her heart ruptured. This wasn't purgatory. This was pure *hell*.

She didn't need him to remind her. Didn't need her secrets ripped open for scrutiny again. The exposure burned.

'I keep replaying it in my mind—keep trying to recapture that moment. I want to keep it for ever.'

She shook her head and tried to step back but he lunged forward and caught her hands. Just the very tips of her fingers. She could've easily slipped free, except the look in his eyes fixed her to the spot. He'd always floored her with that infinite deep brown gaze, but the emotions swirling made that cocoa mix more magnetic than ever.

And for once, he stood as still as she. All that dynamism and energy of his was directed intensely at her.

'Please, Emmy. Stay. Listen.'

She blinked, absorbing the hit of emotion in that husky request, and she knew there was no way of escaping this now. So a moment hung—a beat for breath, for fear to bloom but for courage to be sought.

But then he spoke again.

'I thought about all sorts of... I don't know, ways to try... I thought about whisking you someplace amazing...but I don't want to do that—to use props or places to try to...' He frowned and muttered a curse against himself. 'I just want to ask for a few moments of your time. To listen just to me. Then decide for yourself what you want to do.' He swallowed. 'And whatever you want to do, I'll accept. I won't stop you or stand in your way.'

Was he saying he was letting her go? That he wanted her to go?

His cheekbones sharpened as he suddenly sucked in a breath. 'The day my father left wasn't anything extraordinary. He didn't give me a special hug. Didn't give me a photo or a medallion or a book or even a few words of explanation to remember him by. He just left in the afternoon for work like usual...' He trailed off and she felt the sudden trembling in his hands and realised just how painful this was for him to relive.

'Javier, you don't have to—'

'I do have to,' Javier argued hoarsely. 'Not just because you need me to, but because *I* need to. I know I need to and I want to. But

I just hope you can be patient with me because…' He ground his teeth together. But then he drew another breath. 'It was days before I realised he wasn't coming back. Months before it sank in that he didn't want to see me any more and that he was never going to make contact. I couldn't believe he hadn't taken me with him. I'd thought we were close—I have these memories of him carrying me, playing… I'd adored him, Emmy…he was my papa…' He closed his eyes suddenly and his skin seemed to tighten more as every muscle flexed. 'But he just left me. I never saw him or heard from him again. I found out only a couple of years ago that he'd died in a car accident when I was almost twenty.' He released a sigh that was almost a groan. 'I was pretty small when he left, Emmy, but I think it might've left a big scar.'

The hurt in Emmy's already aching heart deepened.

'And then I remember when my mother left me at that school the week after she'd married a man I barely knew, and frankly was a bit afraid of, and it was only a month after my father had disappeared. She told me it was best for me. That I needed to get a good education. That I was to work hard. And I did. I worked so hard because I wanted to please her enough for her to want me to come home. But she never did. I was always sent away. All year, every year. And I remember finally going there for brief holidays and seeing the family photos of her and him with their two sons and not me. Never me.' He drew in another harsh breath. 'It was never me, Emmy.'

Emerald almost couldn't stand to see him in such devastating pain. Because recalling this, saying this, was pure pain for him. 'Javier—'

'I remember when I found out Beatrice had cheated,' he rushed to override her. 'You know, I'd thought I had someone on my team for once. That I had someone I could trust. But I didn't.'

She twisted her hands so she could hold him and stop him slipping his free. But he didn't try to; he looked into her eyes and laced his fingers through hers and visibly forced himself to keep speaking.

'So maybe I got bad at trusting people. Maybe I got used to never saying what I really wanted or how I really felt because, for a long, long time, there wasn't anyone who really wanted to listen. And because I didn't want to feel that badly again. I think I thought I had it nailed. It was easy not to open up to people, Emmy. It was easy to work and make money and be successful and buy all the things and enjoy casual sex and not ever really give a damn, because no one had really given a damn about me…' He drew in another shuddering breath. 'Until then there was you.'

Her heart stuttered, then stopped.

'It was easier than anything ever, to spend time with you, Emerald. And it was so good right from the start that I didn't want to be me, I wanted to be free of all that, to just enjoy being with you,' he whispered brokenly. 'And it was still the easiest when we were on the yacht until it became the hardest. Because I didn't re-alise what was happening until it was too late and then I didn't even know how scared I'd got. So when you said you didn't want to go with me to Miami and that you didn't want to sleep with me any more… it hurt a part of me that I thought had been numbed long, long ago. I lashed out. I instantly leapt to the conclusion that you'd leave while my back was turned. Not because I think the worst of *you*, but because I feared the worst had happened to me. Because it's happened before, Emmy. It's happened too much before and, honestly, there's a scared bit of me that will probably *always* worry that one day I'll wake up and you'll be gone.'

In this moment, time stopped. She couldn't hear for the thud of her pulse in her ears, yet somehow his words landed right on her lacerated heart.

'*That* is my worst nightmare, Emerald, and the horror of it is, I've been living it these last few days. Because there is *nothing* worse than waking without you beside me. Not even talking to you like this now—and talking about my father and my mother is hideous. But I'll do it because I need you to understand why I couldn't before…' He broke off and shook his head again. 'There's *nothing* worse than realising I could have had everything with you only I then threw it away because you were right. But I wasn't just lazy, Emmy. I was a coward too.'

'No, you weren't.' Because she understood. She knew. And now she couldn't stop the trembling invading her limbs. Her fingers shook, her legs, her lips. She blinked again and again but there was no stopping the torrent of emotion wrecking her body. Tears torn from despair to hope, from devastation to desire, tracked down her cheeks.

'Don't cry, *preciosa*. I'm trying to tell you how sorry I am. And I need to tell you. I need to talk before I touch too much, because if I touch too much I won't be able to talk any more and I know I need to talk more, but it's hard and I'm so very sorry I hurt you.' He bent his head, his voice the lowest, broken whisper. 'I want to give you what you need. I want to open up and be there for you. You're beautiful and special and you saying that to me was brave and I was such a coward back to you. I couldn't hear you properly because the anxiety was raging inside and not letting me accept your words.' His voice shook and she leaned closer still to hear him. 'I wanted it so much it scared the hell out of me and I pushed it away. I pushed you away. I denied your feelings and I shouldn't have. But I'm not now, and I hope you can listen to mine. I love you, Emerald. I've fallen for you—so hard, so completely. I love you and I want to do whatever you need me to do.'

'You don't have to,' she muttered. 'Please don't feel like you have to.'

He smothered a growl and stepped closer. 'Believe me, Emmy. Please believe me.'

She wanted to so very much, and seeing him like this? So emotional, so vulnerable, and so very determined... Her heart swelled so fast it simply burst.

'Hell, Emmy, you know it's hard for me to talk about this...so please believe me when I do,' he swore hoarsely and abandoned his resolve to touch little and talk lots. 'Or let me *show* you.'

She leaned in to meet his kiss, meshing with him in a seal that she never wanted released. The passion of the kiss sank all reason. Certainty slowly settled into her skin as the kiss deepened and lengthened. There was *only* this kiss and this kiss was *everything*.

All words were lost as touch took over—and that need to express beyond words. They stripped right there, in the hallway, hasty and quick and stumbling; they were too lost in each other to care where they were. There was only the desperation to reveal everything, to be bared, to connect as intimately, as completely as possible. All the while returning to that kiss.

She melted as he caressed her and then groaned. She understood his haste and confusion as to where to touch first because she felt it too. Clumsily perfect, they slid clothes from skin, and then there was nothing but searing heat as they finally coupled.

Locked deep inside her, he finally tore his lips from hers and bore his cocoa and coffee gaze straight into her soul. 'Love you. Love you. Love you.'

With every echo he pushed—a surge deeper, a thrust more powerful than the last. An almost savage declaration of the sweetest of things.

She saw it, felt it, believed it. Whispered it back, over and over until passion and pleasure coalesced and meant words would no longer form. All that could escape were sighs of delight—and then, with a final tight arch of her body and a fierce push of his, there was only the scream of ecstasy.

She stroked her fingers over his sweat-slicked back as he lay slumped over her. She loved their shared loss of power and she lay contently pillowing him.

Eventually he rolled, pulling her close to cradle her head on his chest.

'I'm sorry I ripped up at you. I just lost it. I'm sorry I couldn't figure this out sooner.' He groaned. 'But you believe me now?'

She nodded. 'I want to believe you so much.'

He kissed away her tears. 'It'll happen. The heartache will ease.' He swallowed. 'But I know now how it lingers, doesn't it? The fear.'

She nodded. 'It lurks, yes, hiding away, ready to strike. But we blast it away with the heat, right?'

'We do.' He rolled to his feet with a growl. 'But we'd better move for now. Luke will be back soon.'

Her heart soared all over again. She couldn't wait to cradle their baby together.

'I would do anything I thought was best for him, wouldn't you?' She grabbed Javier's hand and turned him to face her.

He nodded. 'Of course.'

'So maybe they really did think they were doing what was best for you?' She reached up and wrapped her arms around his shoulders. 'Maybe your father didn't want to stand in the way of your mother's happiness, and maybe he thought you really would be better with her or that you were young enough to forget him. And maybe...' She sighed. 'Maybe your mother really believed the boarding school would be better for you—that it would stretch you academically and give you space to adjust to a new man in her life? Or that it may even protect you a little?'

His smile was both tender and a touch distressed. 'You really do want to believe the best in people, don't you?'

'But isn't it possible? Don't you look at Luke and know that you would sacrifice whatever you thought was necessary to give him the best possible chances?'

Javier looked thoughtful. 'Perhaps you're right. I'd like to think you're right. But I can never know for sure that's what my father was thinking, Emmy.'

She nodded sadly. 'Then know this: *I* love you. And I will *never* leave you.'

His kiss was so passionate it was almost violent but she melted into it, marvelling as she felt him shuddering with need and emotion.

'Shower,' he choked.

She held his hand and led him into the large

bathroom suite. Javier swiftly flicked various levers in the massive shower space and, once satisfied with the temperature blasting from the several heads, he turned and led her under the warm streams of water. They leaned together beneath the fall. It was heavenly—as if all their old hurts were washing away. He lathered soap and rubbed her down and kissed her sweetly until it wasn't just her skin that felt radiant and fresh and happy, it was her soul.

'I was wrong when I said I didn't care about what your family did. I care about the effect they had on *you*. How they made you feel. I'm sorry I didn't listen well enough before.' He held her tightly in his arms. 'You know, if you ever want to go back and face them or challenge them or anything—even if you just want to return there for a while—I'll go with you. I'll always go with you—wherever you want or need to go. I'll be there too.'

'Right now I just want to be with you.' She shook. 'I need you.'

'I need you too,' he muttered. 'I spent every second of these last few days wondering— what you're thinking, whether you were still here, whether you missed me as much as I did you. Wishing you were right beside me so I could share something that just happened with Luke…missing *this*.' He caressed her curves the way he knew made her tremble. But he didn't stop talking, didn't let the desire take over before he'd said what he needed to say. 'I see now I didn't want to let anyone get close. But Luke has my heart in his little fist and I'm a hostage to fortune where he's concerned. But I'll always be there for him.' He held her hips and breathed right against her mouth. 'But you have a power to hurt me like no one *ever* has. You annihilate me, Emerald.'

'I wouldn't ever want to hurt you.'

'I know. Because I feel the same about you. I hurt you and it's the worst. Trust me, Emerald. I won't make that mistake again.'

Finally, finally she was beginning to believe it.

He must've read it in her eyes because he suddenly smiled—a light lifting his expression and making him more rakishly gorgeous than ever. 'You know, you had me from that very first night.'

She chuckled. 'I know I had a particular part of your attention.'

He framed the side of her face with his palm. 'You had all of it, it's just that neither of us was willing to recognise or accept it at the time.' He drew in a breath and leaned closer. 'But why do you think I went back to the island?'

'For the same reason you went there in the first place. The same reason as anyone—to explore paradise.'

He shook his head. 'Why do you think I invested in that particular property? Why that hotel?'

'Because you wanted to refurbish it—you like building beautiful things in beautiful places.'

'Why else?'

'Because it's in a place that's part of your heritage. And you wanted to feel connected to the land?'

'That answer is the one I've given to others as the most personal I could bear to utter before now. But why most of all?'

She didn't speak; there was another lump in her throat making it impossible to.

'You didn't think that it was because I had the best night of my life there and I wanted to remember it? Because I wanted to make the property as beautiful as my memory of it was? Because it was the one thing from that night that I *could* capture? Because I'd lost you.' He shuddered in her arms. 'But it brought you back to me. You take photographs...but that place was my aide-memoire for *you*.' He gazed down at her. 'This is my home.' He put his hand over her heart. 'Right here. Wherever you are. With you and with Luke.'

'He's our treasure.'

'Sure is.' He breathed against her skin, his lips gifting little kisses as he told her his truth again. 'And the beautiful dragon wasn't protecting the treasure, she *is* the treasure. You've given me the greatest joy in my life and I know that there's more to be had with you. I don't want to miss out on you, *preciosa. You're* the magic in my life.'

When he let go and dropped his defences, he *really* dropped them. And Emerald flew right into his embrace—right into his heart. She poured her soul into his kiss until he staggered and spun her back to the wall so he could brace them both.

'I got hung up on things lasting—not lasting,' he panted. 'Forgetting that anything can happen at any time. And you were right, it was an excuse to be lazy. To avoid commitment. There's only the now—the snap of *this* moment,' he growled and thrust hard, claiming her again completely. 'And I don't want to have just this one. But *all* the moments I'm given, I want to share every one of them with you.'

Emmy fell deeper into the well of his warmth. Shivers of delight—of certainty—wracked her body as she realised the absolute pleasure of loving and of being loved was finally theirs together. It was the sweetest relief ever. She'd never imagined life could be so very wonderful. But it was—and it *would* be, for every moment to come.

CHAPTER FIFTEEN

Three years later

EMMY HOISTED THE strap more firmly over her shoulder and walked down the corridor to the pool deck, pausing the second the occupants of the shaded sofa came into view. Her bones melted and she only just scraped enough energy to stealthily fish the camera from her bag to snap the moment.

Javier Torres and his mini-me, Luke, were sprawled across the soft navy cushions. Both wore swim shorts, their tanned, slightly sandy limbs akimbo, their dark lashes long, their breathing deep. The two of them were breathtakingly gorgeous in their own ways and causing serious damage to the regularity of Emmy's heart. But she had time to take only the one picture before Javier stirred, somehow sensing he and Luke were no longer alone.

'Hey.' She lowered the lens and smiled at him.

The light that ignited in his eyes swelled her already full heart to bursting.

'You're back already?' he whispered and carefully sat up so as not to disturb their sleeping son. 'Did I sleep through the helicopter?'

Emmy nodded. 'Shows how tired you are when you can sleep through that racket.'

'Hell, yes.' Javier stretched his back and gestured for her to lie with them. 'It's been busy. We swam for hours this morning.'

Luke had just turned four and he was a little sponge, soaking up the experiences they were so lucky to be able to give him.

'Mamá?' Luke stirred and blinked. 'I saw a land iguana. There aren't as many of those as the marine ones.' He earnestly told her the most important things the second he realised she was there. 'And there were *lots* of sea lions.'

'Were there?' She hugged him. 'That's wonderful.'

Where other children his age had an encyclopaedic knowledge of dinosaurs, Luke had an insatiable appetite for information about the unique creatures of the Galapagos. This trip they were working their way around a couple of the outer islands, stopping often to swim at the stunning bays.

'Hopefully we'll see some more later.' She kissed his forehead.

'Are you staying now?'

'Yes.'

She'd hopped to Santa Cruz just for the night to welcome the new intake of Flores Foundation volunteers she'd recruited. Nowadays she worked part-time in that capacity, fitting in some photography when she could, depending on where they were travelling to next.

Javier had taken out his phone briefly and a moment later Thomas appeared on the back deck below.

'Luke?' the nanny called cheerily. 'Would you like to come to the galley so we can make something for afternoon tea?'

'I'm going to make *milhojas*. With peaches.' Luke beamed at her. 'It's your favourite.'

'It is and I would love to have some when you've finished.' The peach and pastry treat was delicious.

Luke toddled off with serious enthusiasm. From her vantage point on the deck overlooking the rear of the boat she watched him meet up with Thomas and the two of them disappeared inside. As Emmy turned back she caught her husband's intense gaze on her.

'Are you feeling okay, *preciosa*?' he whispered.

'I'm a bit tired too. This baby dragon of ours didn't let me sleep much last night.' She was six months pregnant and starting to feel it.

Javier placed his hand on her round belly and gently rubbed—gorgeously attentive. Well, just gorgeous. 'Then we should take advantage of Luke's industrious moment and have some quiet time ourselves.'

'Quiet time?' She chuckled, but she was melting already.

His answering smile flooded her with that warmth and security.

In the privacy of the master suite he turned to her—all remnants of sleepiness banished from his eyes by the dark burn of desire.

'I missed you.' He pulled her to him, sweeping his broad hands over her body. 'Missed every inch, every minute.'

She pressed closer against him, seeking his heat and hard welcome. She adored his strength and passion. 'So you're saying you missed my body?' she teased.

'God, yes.' He kissed her—teasing her lips with his tongue before taking full possession of her mouth. Only when she moaned with reciprocal need did he lift his head to gaze into her eyes. 'And your sass. And your spirit... *preciosa.*'

'It was only one night.'

'It was an eternity.'

He took his time to tease her, touching every way he knew that drove her crazy—tormenting her with playful, loving fervour until she was gasping for air and restlessly seeking to drive him as wild as he made her.

'Javier—'

'I want this too much to have it over too soon.' He tantalised with playful authority that only ignited her more.

For she wanted it too—this sweet, hot slide of happiness encapsulated in movement and murmurings. In moments like these—so many moments—of vitality and humour and joy.

'It's not ever going to be over,' she vowed, switching to rise above him and ride them both to that infinite source of pleasure.

'No,' he agreed, reaching up to cup her face and give her the source of balance she needed. 'Because I love you, I love this with you, and I love what we've created…right here. Right *now*.' He shuddered as he powerfully thrust up beneath her and drove his message home— deep into her heart. 'And the beautiful thing is, it's *always* now.'

'So you'll love me for a lifetime?'

'You know it.'

As they soared together and then finally rested in tender completion, his whispers soothed the fiery old scars on her soul. She was no longer alone and isolated and afraid of someone seeing her truth. He loved her as she was. He saw and celebrated her, as she did him.

She held his hand and pressed it to her chest so he could feel the regular beat of her heart. 'You know you're locked in here with me.'

'Good.' He kissed her again. 'There's nowhere else I'd want to be.'

On the edge of the earth, she found the safest of places—in the magic of his heart.

* * * * *

LET'S TALK
Romance

For exclusive extracts, competitions
and special offers, find us online:

f facebook.com/millsandboon

⊙ @millsandboonuk

🐦 @millsandboon

Or get in touch on 0844 844 1351*

For all the latest titles coming soon,
visit millsandboon.co.uk/nextmonth

Want even more
ROMANCE?

Join our bookclub today!

'Mills & Boon books, the perfect way to escape for an hour or so.'

Miss W. Dyer

'Excellent service, promptly delivered and very good subscription choices.'

Miss A. Pearson

'You get fantastic special offers and the chance to get books before they hit the shops'

Mrs V. Hall

Visit millsandbook.co.uk/Bookclub and save on brand new books.

MILLS & BOON